# PASSAGE

# PAS

KHARY

# SAGE

A NOVEL

## LAZARRE-WHITE

SEVEN STORIES PRESS
New York • Oakland • London

A Seven Stories Press First Edition

Seven Stories Press
140 Watts Street
New York, NY 10013
www.sevenstories.com

College professors and high school and middle school teachers may order free examination copies of Seven Stories Press titles. To order, visit http://www.sevenstories.com/textbook or send a fax on school letterhead to (212) 226-1411.

Library of Congress Cataloging-in-Publication Data

Names: Lazarre-White, Khary, author.
Title: Passage : a novel / Khary Lazarre-White.
Description: A Seven Stories Press First Edition. | New York : Seven Stories Press, 2017.
Identifiers: LCCN 2017001142 (print) | LCCN 2017021833 (ebook) | ISBN 9781609807849 (E-book) | ISBN 9781609807832 (hardback)
Subjects: LCSH: African American young men--Fiction. | BISAC: FICTION / African American / General. | FICTION / Coming of Age. | FICTION / Literary. | GSAFD: Bildungsromans.
Classification: LCC PS3612.A979 (ebook) | LCC PS3612.A979 P37 2017 (print) | DDC 813/.6--dc23
LC record available at https://lccn.loc.gov/2017001142

Printed in the United States

9 8 7 6 5 4 3 2 1

*Dedicated to:*

my father, Douglas Hughes White
my mother, Jane Lazarre
my brother, Adam Lazarre-White
and
my grandmother, Lois Meadows White

My memory stammers; but my soul is a witness.

—JAMES BALDWIN

The interpretation of our reality through patterns
not our own, serves only to make us ever more unknown,
ever less free, ever more solitary.

—GABRIEL GARCÍA MÁRQUEZ

# CHAPTER 1

*T*his here is the story of a man. It is the story of a man who could fly, or believed he could, all depends on who you ask. This is the story of a man and his dreams. His name was Midnight Blue, and he was a man. Blue measured about six foot four, he was as slim as sugarcane, and he walked with the lanky lope of an aged but deadly wolf. He was so thin that his collar was always rumpled, bein' that his neck couldn't fill out his shirt. But could that man wear a suit. He was smooth, like a shadow. He always wore his dark brown hat, with the rim bent, ever so slightly cocked to the side. He walked slow as could be, like he had all the time in the world, which he did.

See, no one knew when Midnight was born—he just appeared one day, over thirty years ago, lookin' just the same as he do today. They say he walked from Mississippi, but I hear he might a come from down deep in Louisiana. Folks say he meddle with that

*Voodoo, but you know how folks talk. They say that 'cause he's so good at what he does. He's a gambler, and until you seen what cards can do in Midnight Blue's hands, you ain't seen no cards. This man takes the gamble outta gamblin'. He'll sit in your house, play with your cards, by your rules, and still win every damn time. It's like him and those cards have known each other for alotta years, and they on real good terms. That's why folk say he come from Voodoo Land, 'cause those cards must talk to him, whisperin' in his ear where they gonna fall. Blue's that good.*

*Now, he might a walked to the Crossroads and sold his soul, or he might really know somethin' about Voodoo, but one thing I know for sure, he ain't no cheater. In fact, last man that called Midnight Blue a cheater took one look from Blue, and his ebony black eyes, and ran hisself to the swamp, ravin' mad. That man got lost and wolves took to his body. Way off in the distance you could hear his screams that night, somethin' awful. Blue ain't been 'cused a cheatin' since.*

*They say that man saw into Blue's ebony eyes, and beneath his blue-black skin. They say he saw his own worst fears, his nightmares, come to life. That's why folk say that Midnight Blue ain't named for his dark, blue-black skin, but instead for the midnight he can bring. A midnight so dark that it can erase a man's mind, leavin' nothin' but the haunted songs of Delta Bluesmen who done sold their soul at the Crossroads, and now are cryin' out for its return . . .*

It had been the same for years now. Warrior woke up angry. Just plain old surly mean. Angry at existence. He always knew that he had just awakened from exhausting nightmares, but he never remembered his dreams. He knew he was tired . . . and angry.

*Pain is so damn hard.*
*Well, do you want to live or die?*
*I don't know . . . you tell me . . .*
*So you want to die?*
*It isn't about what I want . . .*

As each word echoed through his mind, Warrior slowly pulled himself up and went to take a shower.

He turned the water on hot, letting the steam rise, then paid tribute to his daily ritual of strengthening. The water ran through his eyes, covered his face, and warmed him. He allowed it to do what water does: breathe life into his body. He listened intently as his anger washed away and he heard the words of evil spirits drown. When he finally stepped out, his eyes were bloodshot—testimony to his struggle. Back in his room Warrior slowly dried off and began to dress.

He chose his clothes carefully. He understood that he had to dress smooth, but not too smooth. His clothes always matched; his shoes and his shirt the same color, in deference to the style of the day. Warrior never dressed to attract attention, or conflict. He never wore name brands or clothing with the designer's mark placed in a conspicuous way. He wore colors that allowed him to blend in, to lie low. His clothes were the only thing that gave him some sense of camouflage; nondescript earth colors were his cloak.

The perfect armor is that of the chameleon, you can't strike what you can't see. Warrior sought some, any, protection from the ever-present eyes. A well-worn hood always gives some relief. People can still stare, they can still watch you, but they can't invade your space in the same way. They can't turn their accusing eyes on you, announcing that they know what you are . . .

*You don't know me. That's why you stare so damn hard, 'cause you trying to understand me. Understand your fear and it will set you free. You think you the one that's got me in chains, but you got it all wrong. There's a law on the street: If there's something you fear, if a nightmare is on your heels, don't run. Stop. Turn around and face it, fight it if you must. 'Cause only by conquering your terror will you be able to walk the street, because if you run, you will become one with your nightmare. It will be your shadow. Its spirit will live in your blood, and you will need its company, its presence, to validate your existence. You look so hard, but I'm too complicated to be understood in a glance. How those chains feel?*

Warrior looked up at the collection of hats hanging from dozens of nails on his wall. He chose one that matched his outfit, and slid it into place. Without the hat, no look is complete. It turns the tide. Pull it down real low, and now you've got the advantage. You can look at them, but they can't see your eyes. His dress now complete, Warrior left his room.

As he entered the kitchen, he growled in mock fury, "What little munchkin's been eating my cereal!"

His sister giggled as he snatched the cereal box on the table. Only warm milk and soggy flakes were left in her bowl. She never finished her meal. Her smiling face was that of an inno-cent spirit. Her huge dimples and toothless grin reflected love and trust. She had cleaned up with money from the "Tooth Fairy." With her quarters she bought more candy, which only rotted more teeth, and she slowly became a toothless, rich candy maven.

Their father had once said to Warrior when he was younger, "There's blood . . . and then there's strangers. "

Warrior always remembered those words. They were verses in his self-made holy book. His mother made sure that Warrior continued to feel those words. She always said to him, "A man is only a man if he shows his love to those he loves. What's the point of lovin' someone if you never let 'em know?"

That was a struggle for any man growing up. Be hard, main-tain your guard, show nothing, live by the motto: "Guard your grill." These are times when men wear masks. Nothing meant more to Warrior than his family, his mother, his sister, and his father who still lived in their old house in Brooklyn. His life was their life. They were his religion.

*Blood runs deep . . . and only spirits can run*
*with its flow.*

Walking hard through the cold morning streets, shoulders hunched, neck tightened, body taut from that biting February wind, Warrior moved quickly down the busy Harlem side-walks, filled with morning commuters. As Warrior joined their flow, he thought,

*So much to take care of in one life. Languages to learn, places to see, sensations to feel. Every one is always looking for the meaning of life, shiiit, this world is filled with simple pleasures. Spending twenty-four hours . . . straight . . . with one you love. Eating a ripe, cold pineapple, after a long hot day. Eating a mango just about anytime. Holding your son or daughter in your arms in a field under the sun. Giving hope to the broken spirit of a child. Making love on a sweltering day continuously, as we sweat and love . . . and sweat and love . . . and sweat . . .*

A beauty passed by and broke his train of thought . . . "Hey gal . . ."
He returned to his internal conversation,

*Everybody is always searching for the meaning of life, and here, I got the answer, and I might not even be able to use it. Enjoy love, enjoy blood, listen to the word of an elder, open your eyes, free your senses, feel the beauty around you. Here I am, living in this concrete jungle, surrounded by pain, with a life expectancy of days. "And what do you want to be when you grow up, Little Warrior?" How about alive . . .*

*You slipping, man, walking down the street, looking all sad, be aware of what's going on around you. Any moment they might come for you. Genocide and ignorance move fast, you gotta move faster. When they finally call your name, there ain't no hiding. Those two are so bad they'd chase the Devil outta his Christian Hell, and take over. Those religions don't know nothing about these demons. Once you've seen their face, there's nothing left to fear. And we don't.*

Warrior shook his head to try to alter his thoughts. He had to get on the train for the long ride to his school. A place he did not want to go—but was going all the same. His mind needed to be more at rest before he arrived. He put his earphones in, to quiet the conversation.

Warrior got off the crowded train to walk the final few blocks. The school, a massive building of cold, gray stone, doesn't seek to prevent problems; it seeks to contain them—a holding facility that crushes inspiration, fuels conflict, and leaves most who enter its doors with a debilitating sense of hopelessness, and when you're hopeless, well . . . The huge granite and stone blocks speak volumes of this philosophy. Every day students line up to walk through a metal detector and have their personal belongings rifled through. At this kind of school the security guards take perverse pleasure in harassing students and exerting their minimal power. They send students to the dean to be suspended if they don't like how the child looks at them. All too many of the teachers have no training in managing a class and teach a dumbed down curriculum that dulls the senses. Inspiration is hard to come by—and for students who want to soar, day in and day out they are reminded this is not to be their future.

As Warrior opened the doors, he looked up at the clock on the opposite wall and laughed to himself. He knew that she had been waiting, and he knew he was gonna hear about it. As he walked into the cafeteria, he saw her. She was sitting at a table in the back, leaning against the wall reading, but not paying much attention. Her legs rested on a chair. Tall, a deep brown skin, with ancient eyes, her aura is straight-up fly. She is wearing jeans, sneakers, and a T-shirt, always comfortably dressed, but low key, real smooth. Not flashy or provocative, but in a way that accentuates her form. Seems like the clothes she wears are struggling to be closer to her. She's a track runner; no, make that *the* track runner. She's never lost in the 100, 200, or 400 meters. Not freshman year, not sophomore, not junior. She. Can. Move. And what a sight are her legs. Between her eyes and her legs, that's full warning to any man that here is a woman to be reckoned with. She brings laughter.

*That's my girl, not my girlfriend, but my . . . well . . . I guess sometimes strangers do become blood. Wise and fine, and knows it. I'm gonna get her that hat that says, "All That," since she thinks it, she might as well let it be known. For real though, it's good to see her face. I can talk to her for hours and she always understands. You find a friendship like that, in this hard world, you gotta care for it like you would with a child . . . with love and honesty. With her, I'm comfortable in my skin; she makes me laugh and think. Sometimes pushes me where I don't want to go. When I'm with her it's like all the voices around us merge into a dull murmur, and it's just her and me. Gotta remember to be gentle, there's no need to be hard here. But it can be hard to take it off.*

And then she answers.

"What's up, baby." She elongated the word of affection, and as always, smiled at him when she talked to him, like she's joking, or knows some secret.

"Wha' sup," Warrior replied.

"You said that you'd be here at eight, you are late," she said, smiling.

"I can't control the trains, ya know."

"More like you can't control your alarm clock!" She let out a deep belly laugh.

"Yeah, whatevah." Warrior smiled, taking a seat opposite her.

"You know, ya can't keep a sister like me waiting?"

"Why not, I do it all the time?"

"Anyway! Am I gonna tell you my man problems first, or do you get to tell me your women stories?" She asked it as if there was a question.

"Like always, you go first," he said.

"Good . . ."

As she began to speak on their daily topic, his mind wandered. . .

*Have you ever been totally at ease with another person? Completely comfortable in their presence, as if your spirits were playmates long before they came into your bodies? It's not safe to trust anyone this much, it leaves you open. They can wield that bond like a sword and cut out your soul, or someone else can use that bond to get to you. It weakens you as a soldier. But Lawd knows, even this here soldier needs another's strength. Blood may pass on, they may act a fool, they may leave you for long periods of time, but they always blood, and their souls always watch over you. And if you try to separate yourself from blood, if you deny their claim, it will leave scars that will never heal. The kind that have deep roots. The kind where, when you run your fingers over them, they feel smooth and kinda nasty. The skin is dead, there's no more life left in it. So when you touching that kind a scar, you ain't touching skin, you touching death. This world's given me plenty of scars, I ain't gonna take none a the blood kind. I'm not trying to wear any death on my skin. True blood will always love ya, scars and all.*

"What's wrong?" Her voice shook Warrior out of his thoughts.

"Nothin'," Warrior replied, slowly shaking his head.

"*Nothing*? You're sitting there staring off into space, looking like the world's on your shoulders, while I'm tellin' one of my most interesting stories, and you say *nothing*? Who do you think you're fooling, little boy?" As she teased him, she laughed, but this time, it only veiled her concern.

"I was just thinkin' about family, about scars. How do you avoid 'em? How do you love those you're close to, and not get scarred?"

"You don't," she replied. "You love those that are close to you, and when the scars come, they come. You can't avoid 'em, you just go on loving. You don't have any control over the pain, but you do over the love. And if someone you love comments on the scars you bear, look 'em right dead in the eye and tell 'em, 'I got these scars protecting you from the demons, would you rather have had me let them loose?' Besides, scars can be beautiful, too."

"The wise one has spoken," he said, laughing.

"I'm serious," she replied, rolling her eyes.

Warrior stopped laughing. He nodded his head and looked into her ancient eyes. "I know you are. And it's true, you can't keep runnin' from things, or you'll never find your own path," he said.

"Exactly. People are always trying to avoid pain, as if they have some say. Women learned a long time ago that running from pain wasn't possible. It will come. You just have to be able to deal with it when it arrives. Plus, everyone needs some pain. Pain is what makes the good feel so good. You need some contrast. Something to remind you how much you need love," she said.

"Men would be wise to learn that lesson," Warrior said, realizing the weight of her words.

"Yes, we would be a lot better off if they listened more," she replied.

Warrior decided to tease her. "They? What about me, don't I need to listen?"

She wasn't in the mood for games anymore, and so she looked at Warrior intently. "No. You already listen. That's what makes you different. You listen, and you teach. If anything, you hold on to too much pain."

"Please. It ain't just me, all my boys have seen too much pain, that's the damn problem," he said.

"No," she said slowly. "The problem is that they see all of this pain, but they don't acknowledge it, they don't deal with it. They say they don't feel pain; that they're not emotional, but the last time I checked, rage and anger are emotions and they seem real comfortable with them. The pain underneath threatens to drown them. Nah, they don't feel pain. Not until they're layin' in some gutter with a hole in their chest. A gun is the only pain so many of them recognize until it's too late, and then a bullet reminds them of all the pain, and all the love they've missed."

Warrior heard her and saw her pain. He thought back to the previous summer, when on a hot and humid day, she had left the safety of her home, a house filled with a tight-knit collection of Carribean women—her mother, grandmother, and an aunt—to go to the neighborhood basketball court. The girls sat in the stone seats, braiding each other's hair, drinking cold sodas and eating flavored ice as they gossiped and talked and talked, keeping an interested eye on the boys who played basketball as if their lives depended on the outcome. Late in the day an argument broke out on the basketball court which led to a fight. It was the kind of argument that happens every day on courts where boys have tied their sense of manhood to a game that holds no future for them. The fight led to friends from adjacent buildings arriving. And they brought guns. Shots were fired and one of her best friends was struck by a stray bullet and killed. He was sitting right next to her, a boy who didn't play basketball, but sat outside with his friends to escape the chaos of his home. She had fled when the shots where fired—running for safety inside a nearby building. When she returned later, to see if everyone was all right, the yellow tape keeping onlookers at bay told her that everything was not. She could see her friend, facedown, body contorted, encircled by chalk.

Warrior reached across the table that separated them, and placed his hand over her long, thin fingers, always struck by the delicacy of her hands.

"So many of us are dying, and we think we know what life's all about, until it's too late." As Warrior spoke, he remembered how many friends he had lost. Like a war veteran, he carried his childhood friends' dog tags around in his mind. The only thing is that they had never volunteered for any war. They had simply been born. People in other parts of the city would think this was just tough talk, exaggeration, but then the bullets weren't coming for them.

She took her other hand, and with the backs of her fingers

touched his face. "The problem is that even the ones who know what life is all about, sometimes don't make it. We have no control, no way to be safe, you know? All we can do is hope, and pray, that some of you will make it," she said.

Warrior felt the awareness of his vulnerability creep into his thoughts. He slammed the door, quickly. He had learned to take the mask off and on, as needed. He wasn't like so many of his friends who couldn't be gentle and loving and emotional with the ones he loved—but even he struggled with being fully vulnerable. He felt the pain of the friends who had died from violence. He walked with it every day but did not speak of it. He knew that violence trailed them, that simple daily rituals, activities that were the provence of children in other places, could lead to death for him. He could be scared. Or he could be strong. He saw them as mutually exclusive. And so, the scars, like dulled skin, wrapped themelves around him.

"First of all, I don't think prayin' gonna do a damn thing!" They both laughed. "And secondly, this man can handle himself. Don't you worry." She smiled, and acted like she was reassured. Warrior continued, "Now, as long as we were on the phone last night, I know you didn't finish your readin' for next period, and I gotta get to class, so I'm gonna float."

"Yeah, I do have to kinda read a whole book before next period, so maybe I should start now," she said.

Warrior laughed. "Please, you know damn well that you're gonna find someone else to talk to, and not do any a that readin'!"

"Yeah, but I might as well pretend." She laughed, for real this time.

Warrior got up from the table and threw his bag over his shoulder. "Well I'm gonna get goin'. I'll talk to you later, OK?"

She nodded her head as Warrior walked away. She watched as he moved through the cafeteria. Other students looked at him as he passed. Everyone knew Warrior. Some admired him. Some thought him weird. He made many of them uncomfortable. He knew the discomfort he could bring to people— due to his words, his perspective, his "seriousness." And so he learned to keep to himself.

Just as he was about to walk through the doors, he could feel her eyes on him as he adjusted his shoulders, making snug the sword he carried on his back.

◙ ◙ ◙

It was dark when Warrior left school. The temperature had dropped about ten degrees, and snow was beginning to fall. The flakes fell into Warrior's eyes, and onto his upper lip. His tongue wiped clean his lip, tasting the chill of the snow. The flakes were the small kind, falling in a dense flow all around him. The concrete was covered with a thin film of white powder, the kind that warned of a serious storm coming. Music pulsed through his earphones, the beats controlling his nodding head. He picked up his pace.

As he moved through the quiet, deserted streets, Warrior became conscious of how he walked. When he walked alone, Warrior often thought about his stride. He didn't walk like most of the other guys in his neighborhood. There was no strut, no bop. He didn't walk smooth, he walked deliberately. He walked like John Henry swung his hammer. He remembered the stories his grandmother used to tell him. She always said that stories were one of the things that survived our trials most intact. Stories of Brer Rabbit, of High John de Conqueror, and of John Henry. Stories of slavery. Now though, Warrior remembered the tales about John Henry and his grandmother's lyrical sound entered his head.

*That man could swing hisself a hamma. He could outswing any man or machine. John Henry swung his hamma like his life depended on each blow. He swung like he was right mad. He swung as if that stone had done somethin' evil to him. John Henry didn't swing ragged like, he swung like clockwork. Over and over and over again. They say his soul was trapped in the middle a that mountain, an' Ol' John Henry had only his hamma and his arms to free it.*

Warrior walked as if he could see the horizon and it spoke of his destiny. If a man knows his destiny, the twists and turns of everyday life are trivial, and he walks accordingly.

Warrior reached the train that would take him on the long trip home. He entered an empty car and sat down, stretching out his legs. He closed his eyes and let his mind soar, not thinking about any one specific thing. He let it take to the heavens, looking down at the earth, detached, removed.

To others, it may have looked as if he was sleeping, but Warrior never slept. At least, not away from home. At home in his bed, surrounded by his family, Warrior could relax. He could sleep as others know sleep. Anywhere else though, he could not afford to sleep. Even when he really slept, and when he was most relaxed, in his deepest dreams, Warrior's eyes were open. It was something that ran in his family. Some of his people just slept with their eyes open. They felt as rested when they awoke, but they never closed their eyes completely. They would half close but that was it. His grandmother told him, "Far back as I can remember, my folk nevah closed they eyes."

Warrior never thought much of it until kindergarten. During naptime, he saw that none of the other children slept with their eyes open. While they rested, he would watch them, he couldn't sleep anyway. When he was young Warrior couldn't sleep even if a friend stayed over. Their presence made him lie there, thinking.

Warrior opened his eyes as he heard someone's feet shuffle entering the car.

He looked into the face of a soldier. It was a soldier from the other side. Warrior looked into his cold eyes and issued a warning: This here is a man. Warrior held his rage in check, hiding it behind his mask. The soldier wore navy blue. He had stomper boots on,

*Warrior saw blood.*

His pants had a dark blue stripe down the side,

*Warrior laughed at the poor choice in fashion.*

From his belt hung a nine-millimeter,

*Warrior's jaw tightened and sweat ran down the middle of his back.*

His belt carried his long, black stick.

*Warrior remembered its use over centuries, and thought that it must be painted black to cover the blood.*

Under his shirt protruded the edges of his bulletproof vest.

*Yeah, you got fear. Actin' so hard, but you know what you up against. That vest won't protect you from four hundred years. There's a certain fear that pervades the hearts of those who are hated by an entire people. They know that no matter what they ever do, they can never pass through that hatred. Never. Your hands have spilled too much blood . . . Blood runs deep.*

On his head, above his cold eyes, sat the final piece of his armor—his precious blue hat. Warrior's eyes met those of the soldier, who was not used to being sized up like this. The watcher is never comfortable being watched.

Warrior thought of soldiers. He thought of his best friend since second grade, brotherman. He and brotherman had been enemies in kindergarten and first grade. They were the two strongest and fastest, in their class, and so they competed in everything. They were the first two chosen when teams were picked during gym hour, and they ruled the yard during recess. They fought all the time. Usually brotherman would win because he was stronger, though Warrior would never admit it.

They used to play tackle football with all the other boys during recess in the big yard. They would play eleven on eleven in a tiny, twenty-foot-wide strip of black concrete. The strip was bordered by two brick walls, and it was known as "the Alley." The name, "the Alley," would only be uttered with hushed tones of respect that told of the reverence held for those who played in the toughest game in "the Big Yard."

It was mayhem more than it was a game. Only the strong succeeded. Warrior and brotherman were the best, and so, in keeping with the laws of children's games, they were always on opposite teams. That is how children play games. There is no flexing, there is no talk, it is known who are the best, and they are given respect for their abilities. When choosing teams, all of the participants acknowledge at the beginning who are the most adept players, they are made captains and allowed to choose the sides. That is the law. Warrior and brotherman were always captains.

On the first day of second grade, everyone gathered in the yard for the inaugural game of the new school year. The teachers told the students not to play, but they would simply turn their eyes after issuing a warning, knowing that the collective will of all of the children was too much for them to match. As it had been for two years, Warrior and brotherman were made captains. They chose their teams, and the game began.

They played for an entire hour, and after the sixty minutes, both Warrior and brotherman had scored five touchdowns, all of their teams' points. On the final play of the game, Warrior took a handoff and broke through the line. The first defenders were always the bigger, heavier, fleshier kids. They had only strength on their side, and Warrior used his speed to avoid the flailing arms of five of them. He then broke into the second line of defense. These were the most athletic kids; they were fast and strong. Warrior put his shoulder down, knocked a few over, spun on one, and threw the other into the brick wall. Running with his right shoulder against the wall, Warrior saw daylight ahead of him.

As he ran for the end zone, marked by a garbage can, Warrior saw the last line of defense out of the corner of his left eye. Brotherman was coming. Just as Warrior began to dive for the end zone, brotherman leapt too. He caught Warrior's body in midair, and slammed him to the ground, short of the end zone.

The final whistles were blowing, signaling the end of recess. All of the other students were running to lunch, games stopped in mid-competition, as Warrior and brotherman still lay on the ground. Brotherman got up off Warrior and started to run to lunch. Then he stopped, turned around, and looked at Warrior. Their eyes met, and passed words. Brotherman stuck out his hand and helped Warrior to his feet. Warrior handed brotherman the football, and they walked to lunch together. They never played on opposite teams again. If the other kids insisted that they couldn't play together, they simply wouldn't play. Brotherman had been Warrior's best friend since. Now he was locked up in jail.

As Warrior eyed the soldier still standing a few feet away from him in the subway car, he remembered the letter he had gotten recently from brotherman. They had had a confrontation with some of the blue soldiers, and brotherman had spent almost a month in the hospital. He was now in jail awaiting his trial. In his letter to Warrior, brotherman spoke of names.

*Dear Warrior,*

*Here I sit in the belly of the beast. They believe that this is the place where they break our soldiers, that the Correctional Officers are the "nigger-breakers" of today. There are some similarities between their tactics* and those of their brothers in crime of slavery times, but this is one soldier that they won't be breaking.

It's hard to write because my hands are sore. When I first arrived my knuckles were bloody every day. They were skinned raw from the constant fighting that I had to do. The Officers promote the battles. It's like being in a cockfight, and you the rooster. Everyone stands around, cheering your pain. After a few fights, once I established that I would not be played with in the battles, I decided that it was time to establish that I would not be played with, period.

I began to speak to some of the other brothers in here, to let them know where my mind was. They saw that I was a soldier, but more importantly, since most in here are soldiers, I let them know that I was a general. Ideas are so much more important than words, and I told them about the "Battle Royale" scene we read about, I told them that we were puppets being played by the Officers here, that they stood by smiling as our Black blood was spilled. I told them that there is no greater sellout than the Black man who allows the system to drive him to kill his own brother. I told them that we were prisoners of war. Of a 450-year war. I told them that there had never been such a army as ours. What other army has fought for 450 years, suffered tens of millions of casualties, lived through 350 years of slavery, lost their very names, and still, are going to win the war.

This talk gave my hands some time to heal, but it

*also got me thrown in solitary. When the CO's beat me, stripped me naked, and threw me in the hole, I laughed at them. I looked them right in their eyes and laughed. As they stood over me I thanked them. I said, "Thank you for putting me in here, now I will have time to think. I won't have to waste time with pointless battles; instead, I will have solitude to think of the real battle. You have only made me more dangerous." Then they told me that I would have plenty of time to think, years. I smiled and told them, "No, I don't plan on being in here that long." You would have been proud, Warrior.*

*In here, my name is now "Nigger." That, or number 77131-TNS. It doesn't matter how many times I tell them that my name is not "Nigger," they do not listen. I tell them that my name is brotherman, they tell me that my name is "Nigger." I tell them that I am a Black man, they tell me that I am not a man, that I am number 77131-TNS. I miss my name, Warrior. In this dark hole, it is what I miss most. I miss the sounds of the letters, the rhythm of the words. They have stolen my name once, stolen it so completely that I do not even remember it. I will not allow them to do it again. I sit here in this hole, and say my name over and over again. When I finally get out of this hell, I will never allow them to take me back here again. My name means too much to me. I'll see you on the outside,*

*Love,*
*brotherman*

These were the first words that Warrior had heard from bro-therman in over two months. Brotherman had told his mother that while he was locked up he didn't want anyone other than her to visit him. No one. Not even Warrior. She told Warrior the daily news of brotherman's recuperation from his injuries at the hands of the blue soldiers, but Warrior had never actually seen him. As the bell of the train cried out another stop, War-rior thought how good it is to know how strong brotherman is. They can't break a man like brother.

Warrior remembered the night when they had almost suc-ceeded in breaking brotherman. He remembered the night as if it had occurred only minutes ago, although actually it had been over three months before, early December, one of those bitter nights. The kind of night where people die from the cold, among other things. Warrior remembered what it was like to watch, frozen, as they tried to break his brother. Two brothers had almost been broken that night. They had been standing on the corner; the wind was blowing hard, cutting through wool hats and down coats. Warrior went to the bodega to buy some chicken noodle soup and beers for himself and brotherman, and some candy for the little boy who had been playing on his three-wheeler, riding up and down the street for hours. Then the sounds came. The kind that warns of pain. Warrior had just handed the candy to the little boy, who had taken it with a giant smile, when the blue soldiers rolled up.

A few of them leapt from their cars and confronted broth-erman, knocking his beer to the ground, announcing the law he had broken and his imminent arrest. Brotherman told them he was a free man and stepped back—shoulders forward, feet firmly planted. He announced he had no intention of going anywhere. They attacked him and threw him to the ground. As Warrior moved to brotherman's side, one of the soldiers pulled his gun, and aimed it at Warrior's head. He didn't shoot; he got his pleasure from just making Warrior watch.

They started beating on brotherman's head until there was blood everywhere. They beat his head, his slumped shoulders, and his neck. Five batons rained down. They beat him till the night heard the sounds of skull breaking, bone jutting through skin, and brotherman's blood pouring out onto the street. When a skull hits the concrete there's a certain sound you hear. It's like a pop, a dry crack. His head bounced on the concrete as his eyes rolled back into his head, deeply bloodshot. His skull opened up like a cracked coconut, but red flowed from his head, not white. His hand, which lay at his side, started twitching from the pain.

Then the soldiers rolled him over onto his back, and one of them stepped up and kicked him right between the legs. He kicked him with fury. He was smiling this detached smile, as if he was somewhere else. His eyes were glazed over, and a bead of sweat was trickling down his temple. His hair was wet from sweating, and his mouth was open and reaching, like he was waiting to taste something. The soldier was just kicking him over, and over, and over again, in this swaying rhythm. With each kick he would bring his leg back real far, open up his hips, and then with all of his force, drive his leg forward, thrusting his foot into brotherman's crumpled body at his feet. The soldier just kept kicking him, moving brotherman's body a few more feet with each kick, as his crew cheered him on. The

soldier let out this wild, wounded scream and he kicked brotherman one last time right between his legs. As cold as it was
outside, the soldier was sweating hard now, and his body was
limp from exhaustion.

The soldier leaned down over brotherman's body and pulled
out his gun. He took brotherman's bloodied head and turned
his face up. Warrior could hardly see any features on his face,
just streams and streams of blood. He heard brotherman moan
as the soldier opened his mouth and shoved his gun down
brotherman's throat. The sound of teeth shattering as the gun
entered was deafening.

Brotherman started choking as the blood and shattered bits
of teeth flooded down his throat. He started spitting up a mass
of red and white fluid. Pieces of teeth littered the sidewalk. The
soldier wiped the sweat off his upper lip with his palm and
stood up. The other soldiers came over, cuffed brotherman, and
threw his bloodied body into the back of one of their cars.

As they finished up their work, the little boy sat only ten feet
away on his plastic yellow three-wheeler. He was about eight
years old and had one of those huge, bullet-shaped heads. His
big brown eyes were set deeply into his dark brown face. His
lower lip hung low, the lollipop Warrior had given him hanging
from his mouth. His little hands held on tightly to the handle-
bars of his three-wheeler. From underneath the green hood that
he wore to keep his ears warm, the only visible features were the
long stick of the lollipop and those huge brown eyes.

He had just been sitting there the whole time, watching.
He hadn't cried or screamed, just watched. The boy looked,
intently, at the few onlookers who were crying, and then he

slowly pedaled the ten feet that separated him from the pool of blood on the concrete. He stuck his hand in the pool and brought up a finger covered in red. He smelled it and then stuck the finger in his mouth, tasting the blood.

Just then one of the soldiers looked at the boy and screamed, "Hey! What are you doing?!"

The boy just turned his head and fixed his eyes upon the soldier. The soldier went over and grabbed the boy by his shoulders, ripping him from his three-wheeler. As his legs dangled in the air, the soldier screamed at the boy, "I'll teach you to stop looking at things that ain't none of your business!"

The soldier threw the boy in the back of his car. Then he and another one of the soldiers climbed into the back and slammed the door shut. Warrior and the others on the outside couldn't hear anything but the sound of kicking and the grunts of the soldiers. Warrior's jaw tightened and his muscles flexed as the soldier's gun trained at his head did not waver. After a few minutes, they opened the car door. One of the soldiers climbed into the driver's seat and closed his door. Just as the engine of the car started, the other soldier, the one who had first grabbed the boy, threw the boy's body out of the car. The soldier who had kept his gun marked on Warrior, smiled and jumped into the passenger side of his car. Then all of the soldiers' cars sped off, carrying brotherman's body with them.

When Warrior and the few other onlookers rushed to the side of the boy who had landed on his chest, they turned his body over and saw that his face was completely covered with blood. His green hood was thrust back, the sweatshirt torn and red. An older woman, with worn hands, unwound from her head the colored cloth that had held her hair in place, gently cradled the boy in her arms, and wiped the blood from his face. After a few moments, the woman's hands finished their duty, and wiping the last remnants of blood away from the boy's still cradled head, she asked, "Little boy, are you OK?"

The boy calmly nodded his head and then turned his face up to look at her. As he opened his eyelids, the woman released a deep, low scream. She saw that where his beautiful brown eyes had once been, there was now nothing but bloody, empty holes.

Warrior looked up and saw that the doors of the train had finally opened at his station. He stood, threw his bag across his back, and walked to the opened doors. As he moved past the blue soldier still standing at his post, Warrior's hands tightened into fists, and his eyes closed to near slits as he stared at the soldier. Warrior moved by him, close enough to smell the musky odor of sweat and leather that rose off the soldier's body. The blue soldier looked at this man, unaware of the memories that flooded his mind. Warrior walked past the soldier and out into the cold air of the night.

Now the snow was falling heavily. The city streets sound different when it snows. The din of the city is calmed, the streets tranquil. As the white cascades down out of the black sky, quiet falls with it. As Warrior walked, his feet left footprints on the white ground and he increased his stride, trying to make the few blocks he still had to go pass quickly. He could hear his steps. The snow made him feel as if he were alone, in a ghost town, surrounded by barren, empty buildings. There was no one else on the streets, and the cars were parked, avoiding the icy roads. Windows were shut tightly closed to keep the heat inside. Along with the heat, the windows kept the sound of life within their glass walls. The laughter, the music, the voices of lovers, the cackling of televisions, the reoccurring sounds of daily arguments, all were trapped inside the buildings. Warrior enjoyed the peace.

The wind was blowing hard, or as his father would say, the Hawk had arrived. Warrior pulled his black wool hat down over his ears. As he turned the corner, now only three blocks from home, he thought of family. He remembered that his mother had told him that after work she had to take his sister downtown to buy her a new winter coat. At school, her favorite purple jacket had been ripped beyond repair when she had fallen from the jungle gym and her coat caught on a jagged edge of the metal bars. It was her favorite coat and she had worn it every day since Christmas. Yesterday, after she tore it, she had come home, her ashy face lined with tear tracks. After gently scolding her for not using enough lotion on her face, and taking her into her lap and her arms, the only way their mother got her daughter to stop crying was the promise to buy her the very same coat.

With the bitter cold his mother had to replace it right away. Come morning there would be a lot of snow on the ground. Even though he liked to come home to his sister's smiling face, and his mother's voice, it was better that his sister got her coat now, so that tomorrow he could take her to play in the snow. Now between the darkness and the snowfall, Warrior couldn't see too clearly. The street was a side street, and what few streetlights there had once been, were now broken. It was then that his peace was interrupted.

At first it had just sounded like dogs barking, but Warrior realized that the sound had more urgency to it. The sound spoke of hunger, not a mere desire for food, but an absolute bare need of it. Warrior heard the cry of the animals again, and he knew it wasn't the sound of dogs, it was too wild, too possessed. It was the sound of the wolves' haunted cries.

Warrior turned quickly and stopped moving. He slowed his breathing and calmed the beating in his head. He listened to the cries and tried to hear if they were coming from behind him. Realizing that they were, Warrior began moving again, increasing his stride, not running, but moving, fast. The sounds were gaining on him as he reached the middle of the dark block. Then Warrior heard the cries coming toward him. They were the same sounds that chased him, and he now knew it was he himself being chased. The sounds that came from the midst of darkness were getting louder, and Warrior knew that he was trapped. The wolves were coming for him, he had nowhere to run, and so he decided to fight. There would be a battle, he might lose, but the wolves and whatever drove them would know that they had met a worthy warrior.

Warrior looked around, and through the white darkness saw that to the left of where he stood was an abandoned building. Broken stone steps led to a large piece of plywood that had been secured against the door. All of the windows were boarded up, and graffiti covered the gray brick. To the right of the building was a pitch-black alley that separated the building from the beautiful brownstone that stood next to it. The brownstone's striking difference lay both in its beauty and the life that lived inside of it. Warrior looked at the alley that reflected no light, but stood his ground.

*No. This is not a time to hide.*

The sounds of the wolves were very close, almost on top of him, and Warrior tensed his muscles awaiting the unseen. Just as the sounds seemed to come together around his body, as the cries of the wolves encircled his ears, Warrior was grasped by a claw and pulled violently into the dark alley.

He could see absolutely nothing. It was a darkness like the kind you find in dense, overgrown woods, in the Deep South. Even the light of the moon did not even shine in this place. The sounds of the wolves had ceased, and in the silence, Warrior strained to hear a sound, any sound. He was still held by the claw, but now it held him firmly against one of the walls of the alley. It was not painful at all, the claw did not dig into him; it merely held him, firmly, in place, so no thought of escape was possible—like a tiger holds her young in her jaws, with force, but no desire to injure. Warrior did not struggle to get free; he wanted to know what it was that held him. Then a voice spoke:

*Well Warrior, how do you like my wolves?*

Warrior closed his eyes in understanding. Then another voice spoke:

*And the feel of my claw? How does it strike you?*

Warrior remained silent.

The claw asked:

*What is it that is said of you?*

Warrior replied:

*That I have an ancient spirit, and a wise soul.*

The first voice asked, with too much interest:

*We have been tracking you for quite some time, where are you from, Warrior?*

Warrior said this carefully, measuring his words:

*I am from Africa.*

The first voice asked:

*Really, what part?*

Warrior closed his eyes and bowed his head. There was silence for a few moments as he let his memory run. He called on his spirit and allowed it to answer. Warrior brought his head up, opened his eyes, and looked through the darkness. His eyes reached the voices, and he replied:

*I do not know. I have been lost for four hundred years.*

The first voice hissed, and its sound backed away from Warrior as an animal does when in pain. The claw spoke through gritted teeth, laughing the words:

*Another time, Warrior, Another time . . .*

Then the grip of the claw disappeared as suddenly as it had come, and the sounds of the night returned, free of the cries of the wolves.

Warrior felt the ground under his feet, and his heart pounding, he quickly ran in the direction of his building. He covered the three blocks in what seemed like a few seconds. He reached the front door, ran up the three flights to his apartment, and burst through the door. He slammed the door shut and locked it securely. His mother had left lights on for him, and so the house was not dark. He was glad that she and his sister were not home, that he did not have to speak to anyone, that he did not have to put on a mask.

Warrior walked into his room, quickly removed his clothes from his sweating body, and threw them on a chair. Even though his body was soaking wet, he was chilled to his bones. He turned off the light and climbed into his bed, pulled his two quilts up over his shoulders, and tucked them under his chin. His body began to dry as his heart slowed to a normal beat. He curled up and fell into a deep sleep. Warrior slept more soundly than he had in a while, but as always, words ran through his dreams. This night, he heard the cries of wolves.

# CHAPTER 2

W arrior awoke the next morning to the sounds of his sister's screaming, and the feel of her tiny hands shaking him.

"Wawia!Wawia! Dere's feetandfeetandfeet a snow outside! We could go play?" His sister's words ran together into one flow of sound as he opened his eyes staring into her grinning face. "Huh?Huh?Huh?We could go play?" she cried with each word, while hitting him in his naked chest.

Warrior reached over the side of his bed and grabbed her.

"We could go play if you stop hitting me, otherwise I'm just gonna hold you here and tickle you all day."

With that, Warrior began tickling her stomach as she shrieked with delight. As she began to cry with laughter, Warrior stopped. She lay there giggling uncontrollably.

"You know last night I got a new coat with Mommy. It's

purple, just like the one I got for Christmas. I'm gonna wear it today. OK?" she asked, her eyes wide, her head nodding.

Lying on his back, Warror picked her up and held her high in the air above his head. Her braids swung down encircling her face, and she kicked her legs as if she were riding a bike.

As he brought her down and gently placed her feet on the floor, Warrior asked, "How about this? You go and start getting dressed, and I'll get up and talk Mamma into makin' us some pancakes. How does that sound?" Her giggle and the speed with which she ran out of his room were answer enough.

Warrior sat up, stretched his back, and walked to the window. While the steam of the radiator rose up onto his face, he leaned against the window. The cold against his naked chest cooled him. Warrior looked down to the street and saw the snow measured up to the windows of the parked cars. It was early Saturday morning, so few feet had disturbed the perfectly even slopes of fallen flakes. Warrior looked upon the brightness of the sun and realized that the snow was more impressive, its power more intimidating, when it reflected the deep brightness of the moon than when it did the starkness of the sun. He turned away from the street below, took a shirt from his closet, and walked down the hallway to the kitchen.

His mother sat at the table reading the newspaper, drinking a cup of Brazilian ground coffee. She didn't just drink a cup like most people. His mother had special coffee cups, the tall kind that held two or three average-sized portions. The cup she drank from was gray, splashed with a dark purple and green design. Warrior knew that by this hour of the morning, she had already filled her cup at least three times. As his mother looked up from her paper, she lifted her coffee cup to her lips and smiled.

"Good morning," she said, just before she took a sip.

"Mornin' Mamma," he said, kissing her cheek.

"Did you sleep well?"

As Warrior sat down at the table with his mother, he thought back to his sleep that night and remembered that he had slept deeply, but not well. The wolves had kept him company. "Yeah, I slept fine," he lied.

His mother put the paper down, picked up her cup and held it in both palms, allowing the warmth of the coffee to warm her. Her rich mocha-colored hands were lined with age. They seemed to belong to another's body, having been mysteriously sewn onto hers one night as she slept. She was a woman of striking beauty, tall and thin, with a refined, elegant posture. Her voice spoke with sweetness, but with a strength that warned, "Do not play with me." Its tone had been perfected during almost twenty years of teaching high school. She was one of the exceptional teachers. She had the absolute control and respect of her class. Year after year. She would have it no other way. If a student got out of line, her voice would descend and order would quickly follow. She could reach any child, even those with the most attitude. As she always said: "There are no bad children, just children who haven't met the right adult yet." She reminded them of their mothers, or the mother they had always wished they'd had. She spoke to the girls like a mother and sister. She spoke to the boys like a mother warrior. She would teach the boys, "A woman is not measured by what you can get in the dark; she is measured by what she can show you in the light."

This woman brought light, and it guided Warrior onto a path few men had ever tread. The amount of Warrior's love and respect knew no bounds.

"I was surprised when we came home so early last night and you were already asleep. Were you feeling all right?"

Warrior thought about what he had experienced the night before. He remembered the feel of the claw and the sound of the words. He had always had to protect his mother from the visions, from the faces that he saw around him. They would bring her too much pain. He had to keep her somewhat innocent, could never let her completely know. She had sought to protect him for his entire life, now it was his time to protect.

> *I bear the scars from protecting you from the*
> *demons.*
> *You are such a strong woman.*
> *Except when it comes to the pain of your chil-*
> *dren.*

Warrior looked in his mother's face and realized how she had kept him alive.

"Yeah, Mamma, I felt fine, just real tired."

She looked into her son's face and read the pain. He was unreadable to many, a time-perfected mask, but not to her. She had helped write the story. She saw beneath his tightened jaw, saw emotion in his fast and deliberate walk, and certainly, always could see the tenderness in his eyes. She knew his pain, but she still did not know his demons. That is how Warrior wanted it. As a child he had talked to his parents about everything, but now there were some doors that were closed. They felt shut out at times, but these doors did not intentionally shut them out, they held in and protected them. The demons held behind these doors would never fix their claws upon his blood. He would sacrifice himself before that ever happened. His mother took another sip of her coffee and smiled.

"I heard you're taking your little sister out to play this morning," she said, speaking over the rim of the cup.

"Yeah, you know I like to play with her in the snow," Warrior said while looking through the mail on the table.

"And I also hear that you're gonna talk me into making pancakes for you two," she asked, or rather stated, while pursing her lips.

Warrior looked up and laughed. "She canNOT keep a secret!"

"I don't know why I have to make them when you can just as easily do it yourself," his mother teased.

"Well that's 'cause, Mamma, you make 'em soooo good. You make the best pancakes ever!" Warrior said, slipping into the voice of his childhood.

"OK, OK, you think you're smooth, but I'll make 'em." His mother rolled her eyes and replied while shaking her head.

She got up from the table and walked over to the stove to begin the activity she only pretended not to enjoy, Warrior's voice once again became his own, and he asked, "How's your class going, Mamma?"

His mother had taught in the same high school in Brooklyn for years, since Warrior's childhood. Warrior was born in Brooklyn, and when his parents separated and his mother moved to Harlem, she continued at the same school, making the long commute every morning. She said she owed it to the children. As always, a few of her "children" were working her nerves.

"It's going well, but the same two fools sit in the back of the class every day, looking just as mad and surly as can be. Some days I can reach them, some days I can't. They're on the edge, and I know it. Half the time they can hardly sit still, moving constantly, eyes darting back and forth. The other half they sit motionless, chin on their hands, their eyes dark and sullen. You can see the questions running through their heads. They're just sitting there, debating in their mind whether it's all worth it. And if they decide to step off that edge, there's not a single thing I can do to bring 'em back. It makes you feel so damn helpless."

As always, Warrior's mother thought about the few who were having problems, not the thirty whose path of life she had changed.

"There's nothing you can do, Mamma. I don't even know 'em and I know they have seen things no child should ever see. They're old already—and yet haven't learned anything. They're facing things that make them question their existence. There's nothing more dangerous in this world than a person with nothing to lose. They're sitting there debating how to use that power. They might just strike out against their own—whatever's near. That kind of blind rage directed by a gun in their hand. Or they'll find another way. That they're even sitting in your class, that they even come to listen to you, is a testimony to you. They respect your wisdom, they know that knowledge can be their only salvation. It can serve as their guide off that edge, and at the same time, make 'em that much more dangerous. Not dangerous to themselves, to their own people, but to those who have put the chains on them. Dangerous to the wardens of their dungeon." Warrior felt the sweat drip down his back as his words ended. He had found that salvation years ago, but staying on the path was always a struggle.

His mother was holding a wooden spoon in her hand over the hot, greased black iron skillet, and she seemed to let Warrior's words sink in. They had always had these kinds of conversations. Warrior loved them because he could speak so honestly. He could weave his thoughts, his emotions, his poetry, together, and speak in his true voice. She loved them because the conversations gave her insight. Insight into her students, and insight into her son. He would speak of her students' world, but he would open doors into his own. His words were often disconcerting—they were too insightful, too wise, too quick, almost too old.

"But if they respect me, if they respect what I am trying to teach them, why do they sit there like that, why are their faces so closed off to me?" she asked, already knowing the answer, in part.

"Do you know the question that bothers me the most, Mamma? Do you know how insulting it is when people look at me and ask, 'Why don't you smile more?' The ignorance of their question only makes me grow colder, and I always respond, 'Why don't you open your eyes?'"

His mother stopped pouring the batter into the sizzling pan, and turned to look into Warrior's face. He could feel her pain as she saw his. There is nothing that can make a mother happier than the smile of her child, and here was her child, who had such a beautiful smile, telling her that now he often did not have the desire to smile. He had other things on his mind. She had asked once why everyone called her son Warrior—why he had taken to the name. She had named him an Akan name from Western Africa, a name that meant "warrior for one's people." As a boy, his grandfather, now long passed, had begun calling him "Little Warrior," and the name had stuck. Now, only she and Warrior's father called him by his given name. But his father almost always called him "son," and she usually called him "shuga." Warrior said he was proud of his Akan name, that maybe one day he would deserve it, and would claim it, but for now, he was Warrior. He would say, "Whenever I meet someone, they know with whom and with what they are dealin'. I like that." As she looked at this Warrior of hers, who was so old beyond his years, he could see her tears. She spoke to this man, who should have been a child for so much longer.

"But we must hold on to the things that make us smile, to the things that make us love. We cannot allow the things around us, our circumstances and situation, to constrict our nature. True men show their gentleness, any boy can grow old, years don't make you a man. The love you bring during your years, that makes you a man. Don't ever let anyone take that from you, shuga, ever. That is who you are."

Warrior smiled softly, "Mamma, I have had parents who have taught me well. I know the importance of blood and love, you know that."

"Part of being a mother, my wise son, is a tradition of telling and retelling. We've done it since the beginning of time. It's our job to make sure our children remember, and live our lessons. We tell, and we retell, sometimes while it seems our children aren't even listening anymore, until our words are no longer stories to even be remembered, pulled through blurred memories, but a voice that speaks to you, cutting through all the other thoughts and dreams in your head. That's what it means to be a mother. It is part of what we do."

As she spoke his sister came running into the kitchen, dressed in her purple pants and blue waterproof boots. The boots had fake fur on the inside, rubber feet, and nylon running from the ankle to mid-leg. She wore her favorite blue sweater, the one with the rainbow on the front. She ran to the table, hopped up into her seat, and said loudly, to no one in particular, "Pancakes please!"

Warrior and his mother laughed at her words, and at the grin that covered her face, ear to ear. Warrior got the juice out of the refrigerator, poured it, and set the table for his sister and himself. The pancakes were ready, and were coming out of the skillet hot. After devouring their favorite breakfast, pancakes soaked with raspberry preserves, butter, and maple syrup, Warrior and his sister were ready to go. Warrior quickly dressed in some warm clothes while his sister ran back into her room to get her new jacket.

As Warrior came out of his room, his mother was zipping up his sister's coat. She now was purple from head to ankle— even assorted purple barrettes dangled from her braids. Only her blue boots peeped through. His sister was very proud of how she looked, and even Warrior's teasing that she looked like a little purple ball did not affect her.

They ran down the steps, into the snow-covered world outside their apartment, leaving their mother still in her bathrobe, standing in the kitchen. He knew she would watch her children leave, her fingers clutched around the warm coffee cup.

As they walked the four blocks to the massive gray stone arch that served as the entrance to the park, Warrior reached down and took his sister's hand. Just as they were about to walk under the snow-covered arch, Weatherman appeared from behind one of the massive stone bases of the arch.

He had been hidden, and his sudden appearance surprised Warrior and scared his sister. He wore vast layers of clothing to keep out the cold, but his uncovered hands were ash gray and cracked from frostbite. Weatherman lived in the park, and Warrior had known him since childhood. There was only one subject that anyone had ever heard Weatherman speak about: the weather, and so he got his name. Everyone knew Weatherman. He wore his hair long, with a straw hat pulled down low causing two great puffs of hair to protrude from each side of his head. He wore dark sunglasses, night or day, and carried a long umbrella, tied to his hip with a purple bathrobe belt, inserted in a leather sheath he had crafted. He went barefoot in the warmth, and wore an old, discarded pair of black and yellow fireman boots in the cold. That was the only part of Weatherman's wardrobe that ever changed. Otherwise, he wore his straw hat, sunglasses, umbrella tied to his waist, and so many layers upon his body that no one knew whether Weatherman was thin or fat. He was just there. Weatherman stood in front of them, his arms crossed, blocking Warrior and his little sister's way.

"Young brutha," Weatherman said, "and little sistah," he continued, nodding at Warrior's sister, "who stole the sun?" Warrior shook his head and sighed.

"The Weatherman knows," Weatherman answered, smiling. Warrior took his sister's hand, which in her fright had fallen from his grasp, and walked her around Weatherman, deeper into the snow-covered park, away from Weatherman. As they moved away, Weatherman's voice followed them.

"I said, who stole the sun? Ask the Weatherman, he knows . . ." As always, it seemed as if more snow had fallen in the park than on the city streets. In some places the snow almost reached his sister's head, Warrior had to carry her over the drifts. As he carried her, Warrior reached down into the whiteness, scooped up freshly fallen flakes and ate some, enjoying the cold wetness of the snow. He held up a handful to his sister, and she licked the snow like ice cream on a hot day as they walked to a cleared area, where they were alone.

They could almost imagine that they were in a dense forest and not in the middle of the city park. There were massive trees and rolling hills. There were icy ponds and birds flying overhead. Only the sounds of cars, and in the distance the high buildings rising above the trees reminded them of where they were. There were no other kids in this area because some had not come out yet while others had gone to the section of the park with hills sloped perfectly for sledding. They would shoot down the hills on their plastic and metal sleds, garbage can covers, pieces of cardboard, and stolen cafeteria trays, anything that would slide smoothly, bringing speed and excitement. The snow covered garbage, glass, needles, and all sorts of things dangerous to children. The snow turned this urban park into a winter playground. They didn't go to the sledding area because Warrior's sister was still too scared. She preferred her perfected art of angel making, or better yet, after a big snowstorm, building a huge snowman.

They entered the area, and she jumped from Warrior's arms, ran to the middle of the clearing, and flopped down in the snow on her back, sliding her arms and legs up and down, making an angel in the white powder. As Warrior watched her, he thought about the day his mother and father brought her home from the hospital, and how proud he had been. He had been filled with the pride of accomplishment, as if he had done something. He carried her around in his arms for days, telling anyone who would listen, "This is my little sister. Mine." As Warrior continued to watch her play, knowing that her mind was still in awe because of all of the snow, her imagination still trying to figure out where it really came from, he realized how envious he was of her innocence. He missed his mother's arms being able to make any pain disappear. He missed his father seeming like the strongest man in the world, able to protect him from all of his fears. He missed the simplicity of life, his tiny safe world protected by their love. He missed the innocence. As he watched her make angels in the snow, Warrior swore that her childhood would not be cut short. He promised her, and himself, that he would protect her dreams.

The sun was rising and its light was beating down on the snow, but the temperature was so cold that although Warrior could sense the light of the sun, he could not feel its heat. His sister's joy made him reflect on his earlier conversation with his mother—the many children who have lost this innocence. The voices, the pain, the things he had seen, they all so often coursed through his mind at times like this, it was as if his sadness could be triggered by just about anything, as if it was always there, playing at the edge of his mind. And so he looked out at the blinding whiteness of the snow, and thought of the Blues.

*I'll tell you what the Blues is all about. The Blues is blood. The Blues is laughter. Some say the Blues is tears, but that ain't so. That's too easy to be the Blues. When you cry out all your tears, when your eyes are dry, and you can't cry no more, and then something comes along that brings you even lower, even farther down, and you wanna cry some more, but you can't, 'cause you don't have no tears left—you crying, but ain't no tears falling . . . That there, is the Blues. The Blues is looking in your sister's eyes when she comes home asking, "Warrior, am I a NiggaBitch? Am I a NiggaBitch, Warrior?"*

*The Blues is when you leave your apartment and don't even know if you'll ever make it back. The Blues is when you can't look your own brothers in the eye 'cause you might cross the line between looking and staring, and then they might kill you. The Blues is when you can't look your own sisters in the eye 'cause they don't know if you flirting or if you want to rape them. The Blues is when your generation is dying in the streets and your prophets are being killed in your mind. The Blues is watching a genocide occur and not knowing when roll call will reach your name. The Blues is when you have been conditioned not to even dream. The Blues is that I am one of the Blues and still wouldn't change my color for the very power of God . . . Instead, I just stand here and speak the Blues.*

Warrior looked out at his sister playing a few feet in front of him, and saw that she had made a perfect angel. She had figured out how to move her arms and legs at the same time, making the smooth image of the wings in the snow. After many attempts, she had discovered how to sit up, carefully, and move out of the image, not disturbing the angel she had made. She could not move quickly, or suddenly, if she wanted the image to survive. If she did not have patience she would destroy the angel.

As she moved toward Warrior, he could see that her nose was running, and with her tongue she wiped the flow. She took his hand and led him to one of the few trees close by.

"Let's make the snowman right here. OK?" she said.

"Why right here?" Warrior asked.

"Because," she said impatiently, shaking her head and opening her eyes wide at the stupidity of Warrior's question, "Mr. Snowman needs some shade from the sun."

"Oh," replied Warrior, "I didn't think about that."

Warrior picked up snow and made a huge snowball, about the size of his sister's head. He gave the ball to her to roll on the ground, packing up more snow as she rolled it. After a while it became too big for her to move alone. Warrior stood next to her and helped. When they finished, they rolled two more snowballs slightly smaller in size, and propped them on top of each other. The snowman now stood over six feet tall, almost as tall as Warrior.

His sister's favorite part was making the face. She ran through the clearing picking up leaves and twigs, pulling a little bark off trees, and digging in the snow for any objects she could find. When she had collected enough pieces to fill her arms, she ran back to Warrior.

"Here. We can use this stuff to make Mr. Snowman's face," she said as she dropped her collection at his feet.

They searched through the horde and his sister found a piece of bark that she convinced Warrior looked like a nose, and they put it on the snowman.

"Now he needs a mouth," his sister said seriously, looking through the mass of items at her feet.

After sorting through the collection, they found two pieces of wood. Warrior scraped the bark off, using the discarded bark to wrap around the ends of the two pieces of wood, tying them together in the gentle slope of a smile. His sister squealed with delight, clapping her hands as Warrior designed the snowman's mouth. His sister then reached into her pocket and pulled out two perfectly matching honey brown maple tree leaves. They appeared almost transparent when Warrior held them up to the sun. Their stems were long red veins that seemed to be still pumping life into the leaves, even though they had dropped from their tree long ago.

His sister looked at Warrior, full of the wonder, and said quietly, "They're perfect, right?"

Warrior agreed, and picked her up and held her so that she could place the leaves onto the snowman's face, her small hands giving her creation sight. As Warrior brought her down, she looked at the snowman with pride. Just as she was about to speak, a harsh wind blew the leaves off the snowman's face.

They ran down the leaves and placed them back, pressing them in deeper, and then stepped back.

"He's a perfect Mr. Snowman," his sister said. Just as her words left her mouth, the wind again blew the leaves away. Warrior's sister began to cry. Again he ran down the leaves and handed them to her.

"Wawia, why won't they stay?" she asked, truly not understanding.

"They're too light," he said, thinking of a way to make them stay.

"But he needs them, they're perfect," she said as her eyes began to well up again.

"I got an idea," Warrior said, reaching into his pocket. Whatever he clutched in his pocket, he kept within his tightly closed fist as he picked her up. She placed the leaves on the snowman's face once again, turning them slightly downward, and Warrior lowered her to the ground. He then opened his fist and revealed ten shiny pennies. Around each leaf he placed five pennies, pressing each coin on the outer edges of the leaf, pushing them down, deeply into the snow. The pennies did their job holding the leaves firmly in place. Warrior stepped back and looked at the snowman. The beautiful honey brown maple tree leaves eyes stood out, surrounded by the bright copper shine of the pennies.

His sister looked at the snowman and said in hushed tones, "He's beau-tee-ful."

Warrior nodded in agreement. He took her hand and they looked one last time at the snowman. Warrior then picked her up and began their walk home.

After a few moments, Warrior felt a prickling on his neck

and turned around. The snowman was some distance away, and Warrior could just make out the outline of its shape. He couldn't see any features other than the roundness of the snowman and his eyes. The sun shone brightly, its rays reflecting off the copper of the pennies. At a distance, the snowman's eyes seemed only to be made of metal, and as they walked away, Warrior couldn't shake the feeling of being watched.

◙ ◙ ◙

Warrior and his sister walked up the stairs to their apartment, drinking the last of the hot chocolate he had bought for them. A large cup for each, his sister's with extra whipped cream. She could outdrink Warrior when it came to hot chocolate; she was the undisputed queen of the hot chocolate drinking world. When Warrior told her that he would get her some hot chocolate, her eyes had lit up, and since he had handed her the giant cup, she had not uttered one word. Not one. As Warrior unlocked their door, she emptied the last of her cup, burped, and looked up at Warrior, smiling with a ring of chocolate around her mouth. Warrior finally unlocked the fourth lock of the door, and they walked into their welcoming and warm living room.

Immediately his sister ran to their mother who was sitting in a dark burgundy red easy chair, reading. The chair, sunken by years of sitting, now conformed to the body of its most important sitter. Warrior's sister took off her coat and dropped it behind her just before she jumped into her mother's lap.

"I made angels in the snow, and we made a giant snowman

with pennies for eyes, and Wawia got me a hot chocolate and everything," she announced as Warrior picked up her discarded coat and hung it up.

"Well, that sounds like quite a day for you, young lady. Did you thank your big brother?"

Warrior's little sister stuck her chin up in the air and looked down at her mother, "Yes, and I told him that I loved him."

"Well," laughed their mother, "isn't he lucky."

Her daughter's eyes suddenly became very serious as she said urgently, "I love you too, Mamma."

"I know you do, baby," their mother said, hugging her daughter close.

Warrior left them talking and went to his room to take off his wet clothes. After wrapping a towel around himself he went into the bathroom. He turned the water on as hot as his body would be able to stand, and let the steam rise until he couldn't see, allowing its moist heat to warm his chill. As he stepped into the shower, he let the water continue the task of warming and relaxing him.

Warrior leaned against the wall of the shower and thought about what he would do for the rest of the evening. It was cold and already dusk, and he wanted to be inside, but he also wanted to be away from the apartment. He needed more space. As the water ran down his face, Warrior decided that he would go see his father. He usually visited him on Sundays, and his father would come to see him during the week, but he wanted to go today. He needed to talk to him, he didn't know about what, he just needed to talk. Even though Warrior saw his father all the time, at least twice a week without fail, he missed his daily presence, he missed his voice. Warrior let the heat of the water warm him fully one last time, then turned it off, stepped out of the shower, dried off, and returned to his room to get ready to go.

He dressed in long underwear and thermal socks. He picked out a pair of his loose-fitting black jeans and slid them on. At the side of his bed he kept multiple pairs of shoes. He chose his warmest boots, dark chocolate brown, waterproof and lined with wool. He tied the boots tightly and stood. Next he chose a thick sweatshirt: black for the night he would return in, and hooded for the bright train he would be on for over an hour. He could pull it up and close out the eyes. Warrior pulled the sweatshirt over an undershirt, then put on his brown leather coat and looked in the mirror. The coat was a few years old and it looked worn but smooth. It had no name brand on its breast, and its shine had been dimmed through wear. Warrior nodded approvingly and opened his door. He realized just as he was about to walk out of his room that his ears might still be open to the cold. If the wind was cutting hard enough, the hood he wore would not keep the chill out. He grabbed a black skullcap and walked into the living room.

His mother and sister were still talking. Warrior's mother looked up and saw her son dressed and ready to go. As always when he left the house, her tightly held face spoke volumes about her fear of the streets.

"Where are you goin', shuga?" she asked.

"Yeah! Where you goin'!" echoed his sister.

"I'm goin' to Brooklyn," Warrior replied.

"To see your father?" his mother asked.

"Yeah, I won't be back till late," he said, answering her unasked question.

"Well tell him we said hello, all right?"

"Of course. I'll give him your love," Warrior replied.

"And mine too," his sister added.

"That's what I meant, little one," Warrior said, kissing her on the cheek. He kissed his mother too, and began to walk away. His mother's words caught him.

"Be careful out there, those streets can be dangerous, especially at night."

"I know Mamma. I will be."

Warrior walked to the front door and unlocked the locks. He opened the door and turned to close it. As he shut the door, Warrior looked back into the living room at his mother and sister, his sister on his mother's lap, enveloped in her arms, laughing and whispering in each other's ears. He gritted his teeth and felt his face get hot. He thought of the pain of never seeing them again as he closed the door, carefully making sure to lock each lock. As he locked the final one, Warrior reached out and touched the steel door, whispering,

*Watch over them . . .*

He walked down the street and sped down the steps to the subway, taking them two at a time. As he entered the station his train was pulling up, and Warrior quickly hopped on, glad to not have to wait in the urine-filled air. There were a few empty seats, and he sat down as the train left the station and moved downtown.

He was glad to be on the move, to be going to Brooklyn.

He was at peace knowing he would soon see his father. War-rior thought about his parents, about how much he loved to remember when they were together. They seemed perfect for each other, both strong, both loving, both full of energy and laughter. They had seen a lot of pain in their lives, and they had learned to move on. His mother, through family and her teaching—his father, through family and his music. When they had separated it was not done in anger, but in resignation. They still loved each other, Warrior thought, they just couldn't live together. They used to fight all the time, but theirs were fights filled with love, and they never turned brutal or mean. They were fights bred out of frustration. Warrior remembered the day when they sat him down and told him that they were separating. They told him that he would be moving uptown with his mother to go to school, and that he would spend weekends with his father. They had all cried, but this was one time when Warrior's tears brought no change in the decision, and his mother's arms brought no relief. After a while Warrior stopped crying when he saw how many of his friends had no father around at all. He had a father he loved with all his heart, and a man who returned that love.

Warrior looked up as the train stopped and saw that they had reached midtown. The car was filling up, and as always, the seats around him remained the last ones to be filled.

*Don't want to be too close to my rage.*

At the next stop, more people came into the car, and finally the seats around him were taken. So many people had boarded the train that after the few empty seats were taken, many still had to stand. The train moved on toward its next destination.

As Warrior looked up to survey the faces of the people in the car, his eyes fell upon a woman whose soft demeanor identified her as a commuter returning to suburbia. She looked up and into Warrior's face. She averted her eyes. Moments later, she glanced quickly at Warrior, who had long since looked away, and then clumsily reached down for her shopping bag that lay at her feet. She nervously pushed through the crowded space and went into the adjoining car. Warrior slowly shook his head.

*Why do they always think that we want to attack or rape them? They've seen too many movies . . . The ones raping you, lady, are your fathers, your brothers, your sons, and your friends. Not us. They've been lynching us for four hundred years for their crimes. A brother minding his own business strung up, 'cause someone said he looked at one a "their" women wrong. Then they castrated the man, just so he couldn't look at none a "their" women wrong in the afterworld. Your men sure did like castrating us though, musta liked the feel of our thing in they hands.*

*And today, you can see it in their eyes, how much they wanna feel that power. They got all the money, the influence, the nation power, the war toys, but they ain't got the physical power, they ain't got the soldiers. We got more soldiers than them in this world, millions upon millions. And here, on these streets, they can't stand it that they can't look us in the eyes, that they gotta hide behind locked doors, shut windows, security guards, and their money. When we walk down the street they fear us, they fear our power and that drives 'em mad. One a us can make four a them cross the street,*

*we just walking, not studying them at all, and they run in fear.*
*They don't like that. They wish they could have the old days back,*
*the days when we stepped off the sidewalk for 'em. The days when*
*we lived in fear of hooded men in white coming in the night. Now*
*they run, lock their doors, and move away from the cities, just*
*because of their fear of hooded men in black. That fear gets in all*
*corners of your mind. Runs rampant. How does it feel?*

Warrior sat in the now emptied car as it made its last stop
downtown. He closed his eyes and listened to the beats of his
music thumping in his ears as the train entered the tunnel to
take its passengers to Brooklyn.

# CHAPTER 3

As Warrior walked up the stairs to the front door of his father's brownstone, he turned off his music, ending the staccato drumbeats and words of rage in his ears, and reached into his pocket for his keys to the front door. He acknowledged that certain Brooklyn flavor, that strong Caribbean feel around him, and he inserted his key into the lock as the sounds of neighborhood reggae screamed from windows cracked open to allow some of that project heat to get out, reggae beats demanding that the listener dance. He stamped his feet removing the snow on his boots, pushed open the heavy oakwood door and walked inside. As soon as the mighty door swung shut behind him, sealing out the cold, Warrior stood in silence.

A few years ago his father had spent the money to have soundproof windows put in, and they now kept all outside sound where it belonged: outside. Warrior stood still for a few moments, his ears becoming accustomed to the quiet. The windows had given the inside of the house a distant echo, as the sounds from within bounced off glass and walls. Every sound in the house could be heard, from the humming of the refrigerator to the ticking of the grandfather clock in the living room upstairs. Warrior took his shoes off—the rule in his father's house—and closed his eyes to listen.

The sounds of Miles slid down the banister of the staircase in front of Warrior, rose and seemed to playfully encircle his head. All the sounds of the house were part of the music, but they were dominated now by Miles' horn playing on the system, and his father playing his bass.

*I can hear Daddy's foot keeping time, his soft, low voice scatting to the music, and his bass singing the Blues, backing Miles, and sometimes, leading. The air is filled with voices, if you know how to hear. I learned of books, history, famous people and their teaching with my mother, I learned to love that kind of knowledge with her. In this place though, I could always close my eyes and listen my way through history.*

*Heard the drums of communication beatin' out peace treaties between the Igbo and the Yoruba. Heard Asante children's voices announcin' festival, running from village to village. Heard philosophers philosophizin' at the great University of Timbuktu. Heard the screams of Black bodies shackled. And the silencing of the Middle Passage . . .*

*I heard the cries of children thrown into the ocean and the battle shouts of their parents who jumped. It was here that I heard the sounds of history times and was introduced to the spirituals. It was here that I first remembered the sound of a mother's cry as her child was torn from her arms.*

*Heard the sound of centuries of the whip, beating. Heard the sounds of hushed whispers and of feet running through the brush. Heard the words of ancient Black women whose ancient curses were just now coming to pass.*

*It was here that I first heard the sounds of trees creaking and rope swinging. It was here that I heard the sounds of Tubman leading, Turner killing, and Malcolm preaching. It was here that I heard the voices of millions, women and men who had spoken and demanded that I never forget. It was here that the word free-dom danced. It was here, in this place, that I heard.*

Warrior opened his eyes and hung his jacket on one of the heavy worn hooks at the foot of the stairs. He grabbed hold of the banister and began to walk up the dark staircase. The entire house was lit with muted lights set under thick lampshades. The house was not somber, just easy on the eyes. The dimness did not change during the day, the lights were simply turned off and the sun's rays maintained the constant hue of brown. The furniture was covered with dark colors, deep reds and bottomless blues, all of it extremely comfortable, either bought that way or having become so after years of use. Warrior's body would simply sink into whichever chair, couch, or bed he sat on, melting into its expanse. The floors, and the staircase that Warrior climbed, had been constructed from a dark, dark brown wood. A strong wood. It was the same floor from Warrior's childhood, and though it was obviously old and worn, it was neither cracked nor dirty, just smoothed from wear. The house was warm. It smelled of cooked down fruit and sweet liquor. This was home. He realized that the house combined his parents' personalities and taste: her touch, his sound, her colors, his lighting.

Warrior removed his hand from the banister and walked into the living room. His father's head was bowed and sweating. His mouth was open, and his eyes were closed. He wore jeans and a loose-fitting rust-colored vest, nothing else. His feet were bare, and his hands gently caressed the bass. The sounds were clearer up here, and Warrior could hear the voices. He watched as his father spoke to them with his fingers, and Warrior heard them answer.

The place was kind of messy, Warrior thought. He noted the music sheets littering the floor, the scattered tapes and records, and the plate of half-eaten food sitting on the table, the thought of nourishment postponed by the call of the voices. He stood watching as Miles' song slowly faded out, and his father's face contorted, his lips mouthing the sounds only he heard, his fingers sliding up and down the bass in one last furious riff. As the bass cried its final cries, Warrior's father thrust his hands off it as if the heat of the voices, the cries of the strings, had burned his fingers, and exclaimed as if something stank, "Damn! I was f-flowin' boy!"

Warrior clapped his hands together and laughed. He nodded in agreement saying, "Yeah you were, Daddy! Yeah you were . . ."

Warrior walked over to his father's side as he laid his bass down, gently, and hugged him.

"It's good to see ya, Daddy, real good."

His father put his arms around his son, kissed him on the side of the face, and said into his ear, "You too, son, you too."

Warrior went over and sat down on the burgundy velvet couch, sinking in deeply. "And Mamma and little sister send their love and say hello," Warrior said.

His father smiled a smile that came from deep inside, and said, "Yeeaah. Tell 'em the same, and that I'll be by sometime this week."

Warrior nodded, and his father looked at him as he finished picking up some of his music sheets and putting them into a pile.

"So what have you been up to?" his father asked.

"Not much, just survivin', what about you?"

"Been playing my music, wrote three new songs this week, and when I get the time, been eatin'." His father laughed and hit his bare stomach, which was showing the first signs of expanding.

"Speaking of eatin'," Warrior said, "even though it's cold, that chicken and rice sitting over there looks good as hell."

"There's plenty in the kitchen. Chicken, saffron rice, and some candied yams. I had a feeling you might come over tonight, so I made extra. Let's warm some up, and while we do that, we can talk about what the hell we gonna do with these damn Knicks!" His father got up, disgusted at the mention of the one subject that had always gotten both father and son heated, even though he was the one who had brought it up. He walked to the kitchen shaking his head, and Warrior followed.

After a heated conversation about how either of them could shoot better than most of the players on the Knicks, Warrior and his father returned to the living room with warmed plates of food. Warrior's mouth watered as he ate. His father always cooked with spices upon spices—pepper, garlic, butter, brown sugar, and hot sauce were everywhere. The chicken, cooked till browned, of course, fell off the bone, and the yellow saffron rice and bright orange yams were so good they even looked pretty. "Damn, Daddy . . . This . . . is . . . good," Warrior said, licking his fingers.

His father smiled with pride. "You know it is."

Then Warrior and his father sat in absolute silence. Warrior sank deeper into the burgundy couch, his father in the cherry wood rocking chair. In the absence of voices, the hum of the refrigerator, the tick of the clock, and the creak of the chair kept the beat, and his father rocked.

Warrior finished eating and leaned back into the couch. The living room was filled with instruments of every kind. A piano was in the far corner; one of his father's basses sat at his feet, a guitar lay on top of the piano, a banjo with one broken string leaned against the wall, and drums were everywhere. Near the shelves piled high with books, was an entire silver and light honey brown drum set. There were congas of all sizes sitting around the room, waiting.

Warrior looked at a photograph of a smoky Blues joint. In the picture people were grindin', legs wrapped around each other, as the saxophone player on the makeshift stage blew filthy notes. A few feet away on the same wall hung a dark, black-and-white photograph of Nelson Mandela looking out from behind bars in his jail cell. The shadows of the bars cast lines across his face as his eyes looked out in the distance.

"I saw Mandela on TV the other day, talking about how when he was a child he never thought he'd be where he is today. He thought he would be a shepherd out in the countryside," Warrior said as his father finished the last of his dinner.

"A man can't run from destiny. And his wasn't bein' no shepherd. That brutha is a baad cat, one for history," his father said, wiping his mouth with the back of his hand.

Warrior stared at the photograph, slowly shaking his head. "Spent twenty years in prison, and then they came to him and told him, 'Mandela, if you swear you won't start no trouble, if you swear to make peace, we'll let you out.'"

His father continued Warrior's thought, "And Mandela just looked at 'em and said, 'No thank you. I come out on my own terms, or I don't come out at all. Prisoners cannot negotiate.'"

Warrior finished where his father left off. "And then he turned around and walked back into his cell for seven more years." Warrior's father nodded solemnly.

Warrior brought his eyes down from the picture. "People always say, 'That brother was hard.' But he wasn't hard, he was strong. There's a difference. He knew that he was the symbol of a movement. A living martyr for liberation, and his position was non-negotiable. Period. If they broke him, they'd be breaking a whole lot more than a man, they'd be breaking a people. He knew that," Warrior said.

"He spent twenty-seven years in jail to be free," said Warrior's father. "Twenty-seven years," he said through his tightened jaw.

"That's the only hope for this country," Warrior said. "Only a leader with his moral righteousness, a leader who knows the pain of war but also is not afraid of it, can grab the ear a the youth. If someone doesn't come along who can reach those filled with rage, the invisible walls are gonna crumble, and America's gonna see the face of what it's created. The pain's gonna be brought to their front door, and ain't no soldiers gonna have the power to stop it. I'm not sayin' what I think should happen, I'm not sayin' what I think shouldn't happen, I'm sayin' what's gonna happen."

Warrior's father responded to his son's words. "You've come up with a angry generation, son. Angry at broken promises, and angry at the situation you found yourselves in. It's a righteous anger, but it's gotta be harnessed, directed, or else it'll take hold a you, and get inside a you like death. And I seen some that ain't never freed themselves from its grips." Warrior sat quietly for a few moments, his eyes studying the wooden floors, and then he looked up into his father's face. "They asked a senator the other day how quickly the violence and bloodshed would end if the children dying were the sons and daughters of senators and congressmen, and he said, 'It would have ended yesterday.' So when they say that they want to deal with our anger peacefully, without any bloodshed, what they mean is that they don't want any of their blood shed. 'Cause while we been talking, our blood's been flowing in the streets for years, like a river." Warrior's words cut through his father, and he met his son's eyes with force.

"There must be another path to follow besides making them feel the pain we've felt. They can't never know that kinda pain. We've been losing our children for years now. I wouldn't wish the death of one's children on my worst enemy. The loss of a child is a bitter pill to swallow. You hear me? A bitter pill." Warrior's father spit out the last words.

Warrior slowly dropped his eyes from his father's. He looked down at his hands and said, "That's true, Daddy. But when a child ceases to dream 'cause he spends all his time thinkin' about whether or not he's gonna die, a fourteen-year old being hopeless, that's a bitter pill to swallow too."

After a few moments of silence, Warrior's father picked up the bass that lay at his feet, and his fingers freed the music. He stared off into space as Warrior now lay down on the couch—the only piece of furniture in the house long enough to hold his frame. Warrior closed his eyes, released the tension in his body, and listened to the soft moan of the bass. His father's voice broke the trance his bass had created.

"Kila was your great-great-grandmother, on your grand-mamma's side. She was your grandmother's, grandmother. Same relation she is to you, Kila was to her. Kila's blood ran with Africa, she was the first of her kin to be born on Southern land." His voice paused as he continued looking off into space, hearing voices. The bass answered. Warrior's father continued.

"Now the way Kila was born was downright unnatural. They still tell stories and sing songs about it. They say the slave owner feared Kila from the day she was born, say that the curse of Kila's mamma haunted him to his death.

"Her mamma was a proud woman, known too much freedom to be anyone's slave. She caused 'em problems since the first day she stepped foot on that plantation down in North Carolina. She was one a the last of the Africans to come here durin' slavery times. They had already outlawed the trade, but Africans were still comin' in through the Gullah Islands. Folk on those islands say they saw boats comin' in right up to the war. One a those boats carried Kila's mamma in its hull.

"Well, that owner tried putting her mamma in the fields, but she just stood there, talking her language, pointing back over the hills to the ocean. They tried to force her, but the more they beat her, the more she fought. Seeing as she was already pregnant, her baby strong, having survived the Passage, they figured they'd just let her have the child and then sell her on down into the Deep South. As her stomach grew, so did her anger. It was as if the idea of bringing a life into that world made her that much more vengeful.

"As her ninth month grew near, she sat one day by the quarters, sitting on an old log, looking at all who passed by. Here comes the owner's wife, and when she sees this African woman looking at her, she get all red and tells her to cut her eyes away from her. Those eyes didn't move. When the owner got wind a this, he decided it was time to handle her, once and for all. He got the overseer and some hands, and he went out to the quarters. They grabbed her right off that log, and they tied her to the post. The owner stripped her naked and then told the overseer to whip her till her blood flowed and flowed. This man brought his nine-tailed whip back over his head, and he began to tear her skin right off her back. All the other slaves just stood around, hard red eyes watching.

"They ripped her skin clear off, and it fell to the ground as the blood ran like a river. They say she didn't even cry once, just took it, and then when the pain got to be too much, she fell limp, and died right there on that whipping post. When the owner realized she was dead, he got right mad, 'cause she held his property in her stomach. He grabbed his knife, walked around to face her, and sliced her belly open, right down the front. He reached his hand into her womb and pulled out a screaming baby girl. That there was Kila. Born not of woman, born screaming at the world. It is a story of unnatural things."

Warrior lifted his head from the couch and looked over at his father. He sat, his head keeping time, his hands softly beating on the wood of his bass, still looking off at something. Warrior brought his head back down and waited for him to speak again. His father continued.

"When Kila grew to be a woman, she had two children, one girl, one boy. They took the girl from her and sold that child away. That girl grew to be your great-grandmother, your grand-mamma's mamma. The pain a losing her child was too strong for Kila, and she decided to take her freedom. She rose one night, wrapped her hair in a cloth, put on her warmest clothes, and covered herself with a thick canvas dress. She took her infant son, bundled him up in his cover, and tied him to her back. She wrapped scarves around him and her body to keep him warm, and close. As the moon glared, she took to the woods.

"She walked for almost a week, sleeping by day in the woods, and walking by night in the shadows. As the week came to a close, her son got a fever something awful, and he started coughing this grinding kinda cough. Kila tried every herb and root she came across, everything she had ever been taught, but nothing worked. The child's screaming cough attracted too many eyes for Kila's comfort, and so she took to swampland.

"That first night in the swamp she heard the dogs. They were on her scent and her baby's sound. Kila took her child from her back and held him in her arms. She slowly waded into the edge of the swamp's waters, in front of some trees and under a fallen log. The baby still screamed. Kila sat there, kneeling in the water, singing lullabies to her child. His head was so hot that Kila thought his blood might boil, and his eyes had a wild look to 'em, like the fever was running its course.

"Kila could hear the voices screaming. She could hear the trackers following the sound in the dark woods of her baby's cries. Kila moved a little deeper into the water, still singing in a hushed whisper to her child. The boy just wailed and wailed, the night hearing his cries, and the voices bringing their own brand a hell. As the dogs sounded like they were almost on top of her, so close that she could not tell which direction they came from, she closed her eyes and cried. Kila held her screaming baby to her chest. The child looked up into his mother's face, and Kila held him tighter than she ever had, almost crushing his tiny body. Hearing the sounds of the voices and those dogs, Kila cradled her son's head one last time and walked deep into the swamp's waters, allowing its coolness to bring silence to the night.

"Kila stood in the waters a that swamp through the night, and with silence to hear, the men, led by the dogs, lost their hunt. As dawn broke, Kila walked from the swamp's waters, holding her silent child. She dug a hole deep in the swamp's ground and buried her son in the earth of the place that had saved him from chains. Kila stood, her hands covered with earth, straightened her back, placed steel in her jaw, and began to walk. Her eyes looked forward and her feet followed. Kila walked day and night, stopping only to eat and to rest till she could rise again. She walked with a deliberate stride, moving toward what she now knew to be written.

"They say Kila walked clear outta North Carolina, through Virginia, through Maryland, Delaware, and into Pennsylvania. She walked straight to the foothills of the Appalachian Mountains. She stood and turned her head up to the sun. Her eyes scanned the sky for the range's highest peak, and then she climbed it. She walked from the warmth of the valley to the cold a the peaks. She rose through air thinned and wind whippin' cross her face. Kila reached the peak and stood there, looking down at freedom-land. She breathed in deeply, and seeing that the air was no different, she spoke to her spirit and then threw herself from that mountain. She threw herself, free. Hear? Free."

As his father's words ended, Warrior still heard whispers in the room. They sat there, without speaking, his father gently plucking the strings of the bass, and Warrior remembering the songs of Kila in his head.

They sat there for hours, listening to the horn of Bird, and the smooth trumpet of Miles. They talked and laughed, telling and retelling history, cloaked as family stories. They told tales they both knew, and argued about the lies. Warrior fell asleep with warmed liquor in his stomach, voices in his head, and the flow of the bass in his ears, his father's hands still freeing the song.

When Warrior woke, it was a couple of hours after midnight. He looked around the room, and saw down the hallway that the door to his father's bedroom was open. He could hear his father snoring; the sound of him breathing in air filled the room. Warrior looked at the grandfather clock that stood against the wall, and saw the lateness of the night. He lay there and slowly woke himself. He never liked to leave his mother and his sister alone through the night, he slept deeply only when he knew they were safe. If he was not with them, he would wake in the middle of the night, sweating, his conscious thoughts filled with nightmares. Warrior had to get back to them; he knew that his mother slept well only when he was under her roof, and it was so important that she slept well.

*Someone should sleep well in these nights. Someone should wake in the morning rested. If I'm home, the nightmares do not visit her.*

Warrior sat up from the sunken pillows and bent springs of the couch, rubbed his face and stood. It was time to take the long train ride back to his mother.

Warrior walked into the darkness of his father's room and stood over the bed, looking down at his father as he lay on his back. His father's chest and stomach heaved as his lungs seemed desperate to take in as much air as they could possibly fit. As he looked at his father's face, he remembered when he was in second grade and the teacher asked everyone in the class what they wanted to be when they grew up. Some kids said doctors, some said ballplayers, some said teachers. Warrior had said,

*When I grow up, I want to be my daddy.*

Warrior remembered those words as he watched his father breathe, and thought,

*If I live to be a man, I want to be just like him.*

Warrior reached down gently and woke his father. He opened his eyes and looked at Warrior in the shadows.

"Daddy, I'm about to go back to Mamma's," Warrior said.

"Why? It's so late. Why don't you just stay here the night?" his father asked.

"'Cause I like to know they're safe, you know that," Warrior replied.

"You an unusual man, son. Most wouldn't be studyin' nothin' else but they beds this time a night," his father said in the darkness.

"Well, you know how it goes. I am unusual. I am special. In fact, I'm smarta than Brer Rabbit and slicka than Shine. I might not be the baddest brother in the world, but I'm in the top two, and you gettin' kinda old. Know what I mean?" Warrior said as he bugged out his eyes in mock challenge.

His father laughed and his chest shook. Warrior leaned down to the bed and kissed his father on the forehead.

His father's hand patted Warrior's face as he said, "Be safe goin' home. It's cold as a mine digger's ass out there, the Hawk's in and he's mad as hell, so dress warm."

"Yeah, cold as a witch's nipple!" replied Warrior.

They both laughed at the familial exchange. It never got old.

"I got some wool hats in the closet, take one, it'll keep the heat in," his father offered.

"I brought a hat with me, and I got my hood and my thick leather joint, I'll be fine," Warrior said.

As his father rolled over onto his side, he said half sleeping, "All right. Well tell your mamma I said hello, and give that sweet little daughter a mine some shuga for me."

"All right then, good night, and sleep well," said Warrior as he began to walk out of the room. The sound of his father's voice stopped him at the door.

"I love you. Be safe on those trains. And beware of the soldiers."

"Always, Daddy, always. I love you too."

Warrior sat at the bottom of the staircase and finished tying his boots. He took his leather coat from the hook, zipped the front lining, and buttoned it all the way up. His spine tingled as he recalled the chill he had gotten playing in the snow with his sister. Hours ago, it had been cold outside when he had first walked into his father's house. Now, this late at night, it would be downright bitter. Warrior took out the black wool skull hat he had stuffed in his jacket pocket, and pulled it down tightly over his ears. He didn't put his earphones in, wanting to be able to hear the footsteps. He tried to trap the warm air of the house against his skin, breathed in the sweet, warm liquor smell, and then pulled open the heavy oakwood door. The brutal wind rushed in, and Warrior quickly stepped outside, locking the door and resealing the house. He pushed his hands deep inside his pockets, licked his already chapped lips, and walked briskly down the empty Brooklyn streets to the nearest train station.

He paid his fare and walked down the long, brightly lit platform. The sudden brightness of the lights hurt his eyes. He sat down on the hard wooden bench, the kind with dividers separating the seats to keep the homeless from sleeping on them. Warrior was the only soul in the station. The tracks were full of the sounds of the humming of distant trains and the crawling and biting of countless rats, scurrying over each other's backs in search of food. As he sat there Warrior became aware of the eyes.

They were everywhere, and they were watching. Warrior stood up and walked over to the edge of the platform. Leaning over the edge of the tracks, he looked down the dark tunnel for light, any sign of a coming train, any sign of deliverance from the eyes. Seeing nothing but darkness, he sat back down on the bench, resigned to deal with them.

*Well, show your face. I don't hear your wolves, but I can feel you watching. There's no use in you hiding, I know you're out there, I know you're watching me. I ain't running, so stop chasing. Show your face . . . You hear . . . Show your face.*

The eyes remained, and Warrior began to sweat. He didn't like the feeling of being watched by unseen watchers, so wherever he felt them he stared, meeting their glare.

From deep in the tunnel, Warrior heard the echo of water dripping. He felt his stomach tighten into knots as he sought to make the eyes lower their gaze. His head pounded furiously from the steady, constant drip of the water. He began to see shadows darting from the mouth of the tunnel, and from within the darkness came the sounds of wolves, furious and hungry. The water dripped. The eyes stared. The wolves cried. And then, as suddenly as they had come, the wolves' cries disappeared, fleeing into the depths of the tunnel, and the eyes stopped watching. With the wolves and the eyes gone, Warrior's head became clear.

But one shadow remained. It stood on the other platform, opposite where he sat. Warrior stared at the shadow and realized that it was no shadow at all, but a child. The small boy stood across the tracks on the edge of the platform, his body leaning, almost hovering, over the tracks. He was looking at Warrior, but not staring like the eyes. He was watching Warrior intently as a child watches an animal at play. Captivated and full of unasked questions, Warrior looked at the outline of the boy, his long prominent head and his brown skin. The boy stood still, his body blending into the shadows, questioning.

The shrill whistle signaled a train coming, and from the direction of the high-pitched sound, Warrior knew that it was coming on the side of the boy, not his. He sat there, wondering why a child was out so late, and alone. As the sound of the train hummed closer, as the tracks began to shake and the station rumble, Warrior trained his eyes more closely on the boy. He wanted desperately to answer whatever was this boy's question. But before he found an answer, he saw something else. The boy had no eyes. Where they should have been, were nothing but empty holes. The boy looked at Warrior as a person with sight does, with curiosity and judgment, not with the fleeting glances of the blind. Warrior thought of brotherman. He thought of the blue soldiers. He thought of a boy whose eyes were gone. Warrior hadn't seen him since that night. It was said that he had gone down South to be with family. But here he was.

Just as Warrior opened his mouth to call out, the rumbling train sped down the tracks. The last thing Warrior saw before the train cut off his view was the boy's mouth turning upward, smiling at him, in a way he had only seen on the face of his sister.

Warrior looked through the windows of the subway cars as the train shot by, trying to find the face of the boy. As he searched, the train came to a halting stop and the doors opened.

Warrior strained to see into which car the boy walked. The bell sounded the closing of the doors, and then they shut. The train began slowly to move out of the station, and gradually built speed. As each car moved past, Warrior looked inside it, for any sign. He saw nothing. When the last car had snaked out of the station, Warrior looked across the tracks and saw that the platform was empty. No shadows, and no sign of the boy.

Finally, Warrior's train came, and he stepped in and slumped down into the seat. A nurse, still dressed in her hospital whites, heading home after a long night shift, and a homeless man wrapped in his tattered layers of clothes were the only other people in the car. The man lay sleeping in the corner, riding the train for the night, trying to keep warm. A blue soldier would walk through every hour and hit the metal seat with his stick, waking the man. They were not allowed to sleep in the trains. Might steal the heat. The man would quickly sit up, then in moments the soldier would leave the car, and the man would drop back down to rest, his sleep no longer disturbed. Warrior looked at the man, and then at the nurse, wondering if she was returning home to her sleeping children. He turned his eyes to the window, watched as the soot-covered walls of the tunnel sped by, and thought of the boy with no eyes.

His stop seemed to come much quicker than usual, and not realizing it, he jumped up from his seat and slid through the closing doors. He walked down the platform, turned through the exit, and walked up the stairs. Outside in the night air, he pulled his hood over his already covered head. Between the two layers, he was warm. The streets were empty and silent. Even in this city, there are a few nights, late and cold, when it feels as if everyone is sleeping. Then there is something peaceful in the air, an absence of tension. This was such a night. Warrior walked the few blocks to his building and opened the front door.

As he walked up the three flights of stairs, he could feel how tired his legs were, and looked forward to his bed. He reached his apartment door, pulled off his hood, and unlocked the locks. He knew the sound would wake his mother, and that once she heard his voice, she would quickly return to a much deeper sleep. He stomped his boots, stepped inside the house, and relocked the door. He went into his mother's room and walked over to her bed.

As he moved near to her, his mother whispered, "I'm glad you're home, shuga. I love you."

Warrior leaned down and kissed his mother on her cheek, and replied quietly, "Yeah, Mamma, I'm home safe. I love you too."

She rolled over onto her stomach, and before Warrior left the room, she slept.

In his room he took off his layers of clothes, hung his coat in the closet, threw some clothes in the hamper, and dropped most of them on his chair. He washed his hands, drank some water from the faucet, and climbed into bed. Warrior lay there, staring out his window. His body was tired, but his thoughts were racing, and he wondered how long it would take him to get to sleep this night. As he lay there, he felt his eyes getting heavy, and as he drifted, he thought of his family and remembered the feel of the claw. He saw the boy, standing there in the station, and lying on the street, his face bloodied and his eyes gone. Warrior drifted and heard the voices. As he fell deeper into sleep, these sensations became memories, and his dreams were visited.

*All ovah the South there were slaves who were old, and remembered home. They remembered the old tales of Afreeca, and the magic. Slavery was no match for they wisdom. Some called 'em witch doctors, some called 'em kings and queens, some called 'em fools, but all either believed in or feared they power. Depends on which side of 'em you stood. Baalam, was such a man.*

*They say the spirits spoke ta those who remembered. Say they had voices. Say that if you thought, real hard, you could hear their calls on the wind . . . That ain't so, the spirits didn't talk with words, they sang. They sang with they hands, an' they sang in your dreams. They fingers an' palms would strike the animal skin a the drum, an' the words would take to the air. The words could fly. They could ya know? That's truth.*

*Say they used ta watch over folks. Say that durin' slavery times they used ta try ta give people a little bit a peace. Say that they used ta make folk sleep easier at night, an' help 'em ta dream durin' the days. Say they used ta sing words and tell tales about Home. Say they used ta dance right behind your ear, whisperin' magic. They say folks wouldn't a survived slavery without 'em. Say they kept us sane.*

*Balaam spoke with the voices. He remembered everythin'. He was a real tall man, an' he wore black tattered clothin' that always seemed ta blend with his deep ebony skin. His matted beard was short, thick, an' stark white. His hair was tightly cut to his skull, and it was gray, like coarse wool. His forehead was covered with long, thin scars of past ritual markin's. An' on his neck was the red and black tattoo of a flamin' spear. Say it meant royalty. What struck like thunda though, was his eyes. They was jet black, so dark that they merged with his pupils.*

*Everyone remembers the day when he was starin' at the overseer with them eyes. The overseer got mad an' brought his whip above his head ta strike ol' Balaam. He looked down from his horse an' screamed, "Boy, what the hell are you lookin' at?"*

*Then just as that overseer was about ta bring that whip down on Baalam's back, Baalam stared at 'im right through the blindin' brightness of the sun, and said, calm as could be, "I'm lookin' at your soul." From that point on, no one bothered Baalam.*

*Baalam would talk ta only some a the slaves, the ones that had the spirit, as he say. He'd teach 'em words, an' take 'em ta the woods late at night. He used ta stand there, pointin' up in the sky, talkin' 'bout the stars. He would gather the little ones aroun' 'im, tell 'em stories, an' learn 'em. He had his own shack set off from the quarters and don't nobody know what went on in there. Late at night candles would be burnin' an' you could see shadows tinkerin' about. All folks know is that one night people heard whispers. Heard an ancient language chantin' ancient words, and come mornin', Baalam was gone. Some say he took ta the air, but that all depends on which side a him the speaker stood.*

# CHAPTER 4

M onday morning came, and Warrior woke up early to take his sister to school. His mother had a morning meeting at her school with the principal and Warrior had the responsibility of making sure that his sister got up, was fed, and made it to school on time before her class began. After finishing the breakfast of eggs and toast Warrior had cooked, she was in her room getting dressed while he sat at the kitchen table carefully reading through the newspaper. When she came out of her room, half dressed, she wanted to continue the discussion Warrior thought they had finished minutes ago. Ice cream was still on her mind.

"Please Wawia? Mommy will never know, and I swear, I won't tell," she pleaded, using her best droopy-eyed face.

"No. For two reasons," said Warrior, calmly. "First of all, it's too damn early for ice cream, it's only seven thirty. Second, even if I wanted to buy you some on the way to school, I couldn't. Because you'd slip up and tell Mamma, just like you always do, and then she'd get mad, and we'd both get in trouble."

"No I won't, I swear. Cross my heart. I swear I won't tell," his sister said as she stomped her foot.

"Yes you will. So, no. Now go finish getting dressed before you're late," Warrior told her.

His sister turned around and walked, shoulders slumped, head to the side, lip hanging, back to her room. She walked slowly, her half-pulled-on sock dragging behind her, still hoping Warrior would reconsider. Warrior smiled at how cute she looked, but didn't even think twice about changing his mind. He knew his mother would flip if she found out, and with his sister's mouth, she would.

As Warrior waited for his sister, he sat at the table thinking of the laughter that had filled the house the day before. It had been Sunday, and as with most Sundays in his mother's house, no one left the apartment all day. They all slept late, his mother had stayed in her robe, his sister in her pajamas, and Warrior in his sweats. They had made a big breakfast of eggs, bacon, biscuits, and hot chocolate, eating while looking out the kitchen window at the freezing streets below. The food warmed their stomachs, and as they imagined how cold it was outside, they were warmed that much more. Warrior remembered looking at his mother and sister, hearing the wind howling, fighting to get through their sealed windows, thinking how happy he was to be inside. As he looked at them, his sister had been steadily drinking her third cup of hot chocolate. Just as it seemed as if she was about to burst, she had emptied the cup, smiled at Warrior, and said, rubbing her milk-filled belly, "More, please."

They had played games all afternoon, sat around telling stories, and watched movies through the night. Warrior observed his mother carefully as they played and talked with his sister. He saw how she wove her lessons, her teachings, into each activity. She wove so effortlessly, so smoothly, that his sister had not even realized that she was learning. His mother passed on the wisdom of her ways, expertly guiding her daughter down the path. She taught her, in the most simple ways, how to be strong, how to have faith, and always to have confidence in herself. She saw the truth in her daughter's mistakes, and celebrated her difference. His mother cultivated the mind of her daughter, implanting a love for reading, the stories, and the sounds of the songs. She taught about teachings of generations of women; the words that had been passed down to her and she now passed on. The cycle continued. Soon it would be harvest time.

Warrior and his mother had sat up late, hours after his sister had fallen asleep on the couch while lying between the two of them. His mother carried her sleeping daughter's body into her room, and came back to sit with her son. They had watched a movie together, and in the middle, had gotten into a heated argument over something of no importance—the sort of fight only people who love each other get into. A fight bred out of past anger, deeply buried emotions uncovered by a misplaced word. As the disagreement became more confused, his mother stood up and turned the television off, which only infuriated Warrior that much more. After a while, when they both couldn't remember how the argument began, they agreed to drop it.

She had lain down on the couch, the strain on her face evident. Warrior walked over to the record player, and sat down by his mother's epic collection of records. He sifted through the unending horde as his mother rested. After a few minutes he found a record he loved, one that he knew would soothe his mother with a voice that neither of them ever tired of. He placed the record on its player, turned the volume of the speakers down so as not to wake his sister, and dropped down the needle. The record crackled as the needle moved over the grooves, then slowly slid into place. The house was quiet, the streets empty, the windows tightly shut. The voice of Billie Holiday filled the room. Her Blues brought warmth to Warrior and relief to his mother. As Warrior walked across the living room and sat down in the easy chair, his mother took her hand from her head, smiled, and allowed Billie to take her into her world. They listened to her pain, and by the time they went to bed, neither Warrior nor his mother could remember what they had fought about.

Warrior's sister finally came out of her room and walked over to Warrior, her jacket on, her backpack slung across one shoulder.

"Will you zip me up, please," she said, still looking sad, holding on to her fantasy.

Warrior zipped up her coat, clipped her gloves to her sleeves, brought up her hood, and pulled tight the strings, completely covering her face. As Warrior put on his jacket, she stood there, blinded by her purple hood, and he reached down and picked her up in one arm. As he moved toward the door, he noticed an envelope on the counter. It was addressed to him and he grabbed it, stuffing it into his jacket pocket. He walked out, sister in arm, and into the morning air.

Warrior walked down the street with his sister, now holding her tiny hand in his. Her sight now restored, and her thoughts of ice cream gone, she was smiling again. When they came to her school, Warrior took in the sight.

It was a street owned by children. Their screams and laughter dominated the air, the noise of street traffic bowing in deference to their sound. The crossing guards stood on every corner, dressed in blue, with white hats, holding up traffic with whistles, strong hand movements, and faces that demanded that the driver do as they say. The traffic was backed up, cars lined up bumper to bumper. It was the only place in the city where impatient drivers would sit patiently, yielding to the rights of pedestrians. As the children walked, ran, and skipped across the street, some holding hands, some absently looking down, playing games in their heads, the drivers waited, and some even smiled. The children far outnumbered the few adults who had taken them to school, and so the ways of the children ruled. What was anarchy to grown-ups was perfect order to the little people. There was no hustling city here; there were signs that warned, *Slow! Children at Play.* This was their world, governed by their rules. In a city where people were divided, segregated into small areas by the color of their skin and the money in their pockets, this was a world segregated by age. The stores were not of a certain ethnic group; they catered to the likes and dislikes of children. They did not have the smells of the Old World, or of the Caribbean, pouring forth from their doors. They smelled of sugar. They were stocked with candy, soda, ice cream, and sweets, names foreign to all except to the language of children. Each shop had at least two video game machines lining the back wall of the store, and plastic jars on metal stands filled with nickel treats rose from the floors up to the heads of the children. Seven-ounce drinks, small enough for any child to finish, found only in these places, in these neighborhoods, cost twenty-five cents. These two blocks formed the children's territory and was their place.

As they moved down the street toward the entrance of the school, Warrior's sister scrunched up her face, stared ahead and shook her head violently. Warrior's eyes scanned the crowded street of the school to see where her face was directed, but his eyes couldn't find the intended mark. He looked down at his sister and laughed at the evil expression on her face.

"Who is that for?" Warrior asked.

"That stupid-headed boy over there," his sister replied with fury, exhaling and breathing heavily.

"Who?" Warrior said, still not seeing the boy.

"There. On the steps. The ugly one." His sister pointed out a small boy who had a devilish grin on his face.

"Why don't you like him?" asked Warrior. "What did he do to you?"

"He makes dumb faces at me, pulls my braids, and pushes me all the time," she said, with hatred in her voice and a fast-developing screw face.

"He probably likes you," laughed Warrior.

"Well, I don't like him. He bothers me too much," she said as they walked up to the steps.

"Want me to set 'im straight?" Warrior asked, looking into

his sister's face. She nodded her head up and down so fast Warrior thought it might fall off. Still holding her hand, he walked with her up the flight of stairs to the front doors of the school. When he saw her, the boy's eyes lit up, and his mouth began to open to voice his first insult of the week as if he had been working on his delivery all weekend, reciting his words over and over again in his mind, and now his entire body was full of anticipation. Just as they walked near him, the boy stuck his head right in front of Warrior's sister's face and fully opened his near toothless mouth to speak, his eyes full of glee. Warrior cut the boy's words off before they left his mouth. He grabbed the boy and held him up in the air so that his face was now right in front of Warrior's. Warrior looked right into his eyes. The boy's face changed drastically.

"Hello, little boy, my name is Warrior. This girl you've been messing with is my sister, and when people mess with her, I get very angry. Understand?" The little boy nodded his head slowly, aware that he was in serious trouble.

"Now, I don't want you to touch her, make faces at her, or even say anything to her. Otherwise, I'm gonna come back here again, and we're gonna have another talk. I told her that if you ever bother her, even once more, to come and get me. Now, you wouldn't want that, would you?" Warrior gave him an evil look that almost matched his sister's. The boy's eyes got big with understanding, and he nodded again, this time much faster. He looked down at the ground, and then at Warrior.

"You could put me down now?" he asked, hopefully.

Warrior slowly took the boy from the air and put him down on the ground. The boy looked at Warrior's sister with new respect, and immediately took off running into the school. Warrior's sister squealed with delight, jumped up and down, and as Warrior leaned toward her, hugged his neck with both arms.

"Thankyou, thankyou, thankyou! You're the best, Wawia," she said.

"That's what big brothers are for," Warrior said as he kissed her and stood up.

As his sister walked into school, Warrior looked at her, saw her devilish smile and signifying eyes. He saw her detached look, and the way she absently rubbed her hands together, her mind racing with her now limitless possibilities. Warrior laughed to himself. That boy is in serious trouble, he thought. She's gonna make his life hell. He shrugged his shoulders and walked down the stairs to catch the train to his school, glad to have turned the tide in his sister's favor.

As he stood in the train station, waiting, as usual, Warrior remembered that his mother had asked him to pick up his sister's medical form from the school clinic. She had told Warrior twice, and when she had begun to remind him a third time, he had said, "Mamma, I won't forget. I don't forget things like that." She had agreed, acknowledging his excellent memory, and had not reminded him again. He had forgotten. He shook his head, sighed, and walked down the long platform to the exit. He made his way up the stair from the train's tunnel, and into the busy rush-hour streets.

When Warrior again reached the street of the school, it was much quieter. School had begun, and most of the students had already reached their classes. A few stragglers, the ones who had no one to get them ready in the mornings, were still slowly coming in, but the sounds and the commotion were gone. The crossing guards were still directing traffic but with less force, and the cars were once again driving at city speeds.

As Warrior walked up to the steps to the school, a boy came up behind him. The boy, about ten years old, carried all of his height in his long legs. His green faded corduroy pants were much too long. They had been hemmed on the bottom to fit his height and may have been handed down to him by an older brother. On one leg the hem had fallen out, and the cuff dragged on the ground below his black sneakers, collecting dirt and gray snow, changing the color from faded green to dusty gray. His uncombed hair and scalp was in need of greasing. His brown skin was ashy, craved lotion, his hands chafed in the winter cold. His lips, chapped till broken by the wind, were desperate for Vaseline. No one had bothered to clean up after the Sand Man, his nighttime droppings filling the child's eyes with morning crust. The boy ran up the stairs, almost tripping on his untied shoelaces, and Warrior followed.

He walked through the doors of the school surprised by the silence. The halls were empty. Classes had begun. On the first floor Warrior walked down the hallway toward the back staircase. On the first floor were the kindergarten, first grade, and second grade classrooms. As students moved up in grades, they moved up in flights. The top floor of the school was reserved for the oldest kids. The linoleum floors of the hallways were green squares outlined in black, the walls were made of light gray tiles, and the doors were of a darker gray metal. The walls were lined with words of encouragement, posters stating the

Student of the Week for each class, pictures of famous people. What brought life to the walls, were the endless pieces of children's art. There were brightly painted rainbows, finger paintings of dogs, cats, and houses. There were great pieces of white paper filled only with the colorful pressings of tiny, paint-covered hands. There were abstract butterflies, created by placing many drops of paint on a sheet of paper and then folding it, mushing the colors together. Mostly though, there were crayon and watercolor pictures with the same title: "Me." Warrior walked through the gallery in awe.

As he walked, he looked through the window in the door of one of the empty classrooms. The activity sign on the door, made of construction paper with a swinging wheel and an arrow pointing to whichever activity the class was engaged in, pointed to the word "gym." Warrior pushed open the door, and looked in. He noticed the tiny desks and chairs, the one adult-sized table at the front of the class. Chairs like these had once held his body but now would not even fit one of his legs. The tables were more like stools, and the students' cubbies, lined with their coats, hats, gloves, and backpacks, now couldn't even fit his bag. The play area in the back of the room was covered with a thick rug, cornered off by shelves filled with woodblocks and books. The top of the shelves reached only to Warrior's waist. Warrior remembered reaching high for books. He remembered playing games with brotherman, tossing wooden blocks at targets. He remembered boredom descending, and the games finally ending with the two of them throwing the blocks at each other. As Warrior's eyes moved around the room, recalling those days, he heard a man clear his throat behind him.

The security guard was an older man with a smiling face and a large belly. He held a cup of coffee in one hand, and a clipboard with rumpled sheets of paper under his other arm. From the drooping belt that hung under his overflowing stomach swung a giant key ring that seemed to have enough keys on it to unlock every known lock in the school, and also those long-forgotten, buried, and unknown. His voice told of Southern roots.

"Can I help ya, son?" the man asked, his accent reminding Warrior of his grandfather's.

"I'm here to get my sister's medical form from the clinic, and I started lookin' around," Warrior said.

"Well the clinic is right down the back stairs, through the doors, and make yourself a left," the guard said, pointing through the walls.

"Yeah, I know where it is. I just stopped to look at their artwork," Warrior said.

"It's somethin', ain't it?" remarked the guard. "Seems like every child has art talent when they young. They little, but they got stories to tell," said the guard.

"That's the truth. I haven't seen any of my sister's pieces, but I still can't take my eyes off the walls."

"I know what ya mean, son, some days I spend my lunch hour just walkin' the halls, lookin' at they work. I reckon that's one a the reasons I like workin' here. Anytime I start fixin' to leave this place, somethin' always keeps me. Figure it might be the children," said the guard as he looked at the walls.

"Might be," said Warrior. "Might be."

The guard brought his eyes down from the walls looked at

Warrior and asked, "So what'd ya say your sister's name was?" Warrior gave the man her name, and the guard laughed as his belly shook.

"Oh yeah! She's a right cute one. Always runnin' 'roun' here, lookin' to git inna some'in'. Cute as can be! Reminds me a my grandbaby." The man looked past Warrior, remembering his own granddaughter's face.

"Yeah, that's my sister. Mine," said Warrior.

The guard returned his thoughts to Warrior. "Well you go ahead and look aroun', and take care now, son, hear?" The guard smiled, and as Warrior watched, he moved on down the hallway. His keys jingled on his hip, and the sound of his deep, low voice filled the air. He hummed the notes to a long-sung spiritual, and the rhythms bounced off the walls, echoing in Warrior's ears.

◙ ◙ ◙

As Warrior walked slowly from the train station to his school, he remembered how he had felt about school days when he was younger. He would wake every morning and choose a special outfit for the day, usually mixing bright colors that didn't match. He would dress quickly, eat breakfast, and run down the staircase of his Brooklyn brownstone. He would meet brotherman at the foot of his stoop, and the two of them would run off to school, a whole new day of adventure in front of them.

In those days, school was exciting and new. It was your job to play, and playing taught invaluable lessons for life. In those days, Warrior felt that he was learning something in school, but not anymore. Now school was monotonous. Warrior felt he was learning pointless information that he would never use, and it definitely was not fun. Now he learned his true lessons through the countless books he read, the discussions with his mother and father, the wisdom passed down from elders he knew, and the education that comes with living. His school didn't care enough to teach him. They seemed concerned with order, rules, state tests, and statistics.

Warrior walked up the many stone steps to the school and entered through the front doors. It was the middle of second period, and the hallways were empty. He walked to his locker and opened the padlock. As he hung his coat on the hook, Warrior noticed the letter he had grabbed from the counter before leaving home sticking out of the coat pocket. He turned it over and saw that it was from brotherman. Warrior quickly threw his books into his bag, shut his locker, and walked to one of the few quiet areas by the gym, below the offices, a place he often went to think. He sat down on the steps and opened the letter. A cold breeze from the large open window above him blew against his face. He was not the first to open the envelope. It had been unsealed already, and read by the prison censors. It was marked with their stamp. The postmark showed that the censor's meddling had delayed the letter for over a week. Warrior unfolded the letter and entered brotherman's world.

> *Dear Warrior,*
>
> *My trial is coming up, and I'm starting to get nervous. I know that they have no case, but that means nothing. They might convince the jury that it's illegal*

*in this state to assault a blue soldier's stick with a Black skull. Or they might convince them that my teeth committed felonious assault against the soldier's gun. You never know. Nothing would surprise me anymore. They've already had me behind these bars for months now. The charge? Gettin' my Black ass beat. The law ain't nothing but our guillotine.*

*I gotta get outta here soon, Warrior. There's too much ugliness in this place. You surround a man with ugliness like this for long enough, some of it's gonna rub off. A man can't drink and breathe pollution, and remain clean. I'm surrounded by hatred and brutality, and I can feel the rage growing inside of me. My blood is flowing with violence. I know that that is just what they want. That they want me to strike out, to give 'em cause. And I will not be their creation. They brutalize for the sake of brutalizing. I can see it in their eyes, how much they enjoy pushing me to the edge. If I respond in kind, they win. I'm not gonna have that.*

*I'm trying to maintain. To stay on the path. But they've turned it into a gauntlet, and it's hard not to stumble. I don't remember so many of the turns anymore. It's like I'm trying to find my way through darkness. It is the darkness that breeds hatred. With the hatred comes violence. I know the way. But it is so tempting to turn into them.*

*Remember the bears in the zoo, Warrior? Remember how when we were little kids it was our favorite place, until we saw them that time. Then we didn't like it*

*so much anymore. I keep seeing those bears, I keep*
*hearing their cries. I gotta get out, Warrior. My head*
*is constantly pounding, I hear the voices whispering. I*
*can't spend the rest of my life in a cage.*

*love,*
*brotherman*

Warrior finished the letter and sat on the cold, hard steps, staring out the open window. He crumpled the envelope of the letter in his fist and threw it out the window, its weight fighting the force of the breeze. He gently folded the letter in half, and then in half again, pressed down the edges firmly, and placed the letter in his shirt pocket. The bell for third period sounded, and Warrior reached up and grabbed the banister of the stairs, pulling himself up. He threw his bag across his shoulder and walked to English class.

The classroom was bright, and the radiators were furiously hissing as steam rose through the metal pipes. Warrior walked to the back of the room acknowledging no one. He fell into a chair in the last row and immediately moved his eyes to the window. Some of his classmates gossiped, drew on their desks, or flirted with each other, while a few tried to make eye contact with Warrior. Their attempts rejected, the students simply added this latest rejection to a list of many, engraving their image of Warrior in stone. He did not care what image they carved, his mind was in distant places, and they were still busy being here and acting like young children.

Warrior listened to the shrill whistle of the radiator, and felt the first beads of sweat trickle down his neck. The metal chairs of the classroom were too narrow for Warrior's broad back, and the sides of the chair dug into his shoulder blades. As he sat, sweating, he looked out at the trees—their branches stripped bare by the wind. He heard, somewhere, the sound of the teacher's voice greeting the class, and their mumbled replies of "Good morning." The teacher spoke, her voice calling off the names of students, and Warrior's eyes remained on the trees.

". . . Warrior? Is he here? Oh yes, there he is. Warrior? Warrior, are you with us?" The teacher's voice cut through Warrior's thoughts, and he turned his eyes toward her.

"Here," Warrior replied, through hardened eyes.

"Please try to stay with us, Warrior. This is class time you know?" The teacher spoke while looking down from above her glasses.

"Yes. I know it's class time," replied Warrior as the teacher continued her roll call. Warrior shifted in his seat and began to sweat harder. Again he listened to the radiator, its whistle far more interesting to him than the teacher's daily ritual. Warrior listened for a while, until the teacher's voice broke through once more.

"Now what we are going to do today is to work on our writing, using the autobiographical form. I want each of you to write a statement in the next thirty minutes that tells a little something about yourself. I want you to tell me who you are. Any questions?"

Warrior laughed.

"Yes, Warrior?" the teacher asked. "What seems to be the problem?"

"Why do you think that I'd want to tell you anything about me? You really think I care if you know who I am? You can't handle who I am. We come from two completely different places, you could never understand my world." Warrior stared at the teacher.

"Well, why don't you try to tell me a little bit about your world? Try to make me understand this complicated place," the teacher said.

"What about you? Are you gonna tell us about who you are? Are you gonna show me 'a little bit' of your world?" Warrior asked, his head tilted to the side.

"I am not the student here, Warrior, you are. I have a choice, you do not. Answer the question," the teacher said, raising her voice.

"You're asking for personal information. You're asking us to open up to you, to let you inside our minds, and I don't have enough time to show you that place. And then you won't even give us the respect of allowing us the same insight into yours. That seems—" Warrior's words were cut off by the teacher's.

"That's too bad, now isn't it? Now the question is 'Who are you?' Answer the question, however you may like. If you want to consider the exercise one of me looking into your mind, so be it. Just do it," the teacher said, taking off her glasses while she spoke.

"Fine," Warrior said, "but you might not like what you see." He opened up his notebook and tore out a piece of paper. He wrote his name and the date in the upper left-hand corner, and then stared down at the blank sheet. Drops of sweat fell onto the page. Warrior wiped the wetness from his forehead, but that only caused more drops to fall. As he sat there, sweating, the words came.

*All of our souls contain rage. It is in our music, it is in our walk, it is in our blood. There are those who say, 'But some continue to smile.' Our souls are made of many layers. Be assured: We wear masks, you do not see the rage in our eyes. I recently met an elder who asked me how old I was. Before I could answer he said, "Seventeen." When I looked surprised, he said simply, "I can tell because your eyes are full of anger." Our eyes reflect our souls.*

*You want to know what I am? Look beneath the mask. You want to know what I have seen? Look into my eyes. You want to know why I am so loud? They have tried to silence my voice since I came out screaming. When I was born the white nurse handed me to my mother with the words, "Here is your screaming little Black Panther." So you want to know why I carry a chip on my shoulder, why I walk so strong, and wear such a tightened jaw? You walk to live, I walk to survive. The names we wear tell stories of death.*

*You ask me who I am? I tell you I don't know. I am not supposed to survive; I am supposed to die. You see, my brothers are disappearing. Countless numbers of them march in the army of the dead. I do not want to walk with them, I avoid my destiny, and so I serve as witness. If you were to go to our graveyard and ask all those with hearts filled with rage to scream, the sound emanating from beneath the ground would be deafening. Each day, more voices scream. Each day, more soldiers fall. Each day, roll call lists another name. Each day, another part of me, dies. Who am I? I am seventeen. I am Black. I am barely alive.*

Warrior finished writing just as his hand began to cramp. He shook the cramp out, flinging more moisture on the page, making the ink run. He stood up suddenly from his seat, grabbed his bag, and walked to the teacher's desk at the front of the class. He thrust the page at her, turned his back, and walked out of the classroom. As he walked through the door, the teacher called to him.

"Warrior? Warrior! There are still fifteen minutes left in this class! Warrior . . ." Her words faded away as Warrior walked into the hallway, the classroom door swinging shut behind him. The cool air brought relief from the sounds of the radiator and of the teacher's voice.

Warrior walked to his locker. He opened the steel door and took out his jacket. He placed two books that he was reading in his bag, grabbed his hat, and shut the locker. He put on his jacket and zipped it up over his still sweating body. He put one arm through his bag, and hat in hand, he walked down the hallway and out the school door.

As he walked down the steps he saw her coming toward him. Her long legs were quickly covering the ground from the street to the school, desperate to get her out of the cold that she hated. Her wide, thick scarf wrapped around her head and neck, its length keeping her ears and face warm, and her still wet hair unfrozen. From under the dark scarf, Warrior could see her ancient eyes.

"Baby, you're going the wrong way. You're supposed to be going into school at this time, not out," she said as they met on the steps. Warrior just looked at her. She took his hand.

"What's wrong?" She looked deep into his face. "What's wrong?" she said, softly this time.

Warrior slowly shook his head. "These people are fools, that's all. They stressin' me. We sit in class every day, every year, listening to their story. What about ours? They spend all their time dismissing our experience and then they got the nerve to ask me, 'Who are you?' We've survived things that no other people have ever seen, and now they want to know how it is that we've done that surviving. They wanna know the secrets. They take fifteen minutes of one class to deal with me. They think that they can understand what I have seen in that little time. They think we're that simple." Warrior's jaw tightened as his words ended.

She heard Warrior's words and responded. "English class, right? She asked you to tell her who you are? Yeah, we had the same class yesterday. They are fools." She nodded.

"She thinks I'm gonna tell her a damn thing about me, like I'm a damn experiment or somethin'." Warrior spit in disgust.

She shook her head and closed her eyes. "That's the most insulting part of it all. That in this place, we'll read one book about us, have a class about us, and that's supposed to equal fifteen years of their story. There are more of us in this world than them, and our experience is taught as a supplement. Through one exercise, they think they can understand us, who we are, and where we come from. We've had to learn for fifteen years who they are. They don't understand what it has done to some of us. How it can get inside our minds." Her eyes remained closed as she stopped speaking.

"And now that I've given her just a little taste of who I am, she'll probably tell me that I'm filled with hate." Warrior rolled his eyes as he spoke.

"So what does she call it when they've been giving us a little taste of who they are since we were five years old? I wanna know what that's called," she said.

"They call that 'education,'" Warrior said softly.

They stood there, the wind blowing around them, her scarf waving in the air. They stood in silence. Words flowed between them that no one else could hear. They passed unsaid descriptions of what they felt, and with her touch and her attentive eyes, she tried to calm him. She knew she loved him, not in a light surface kind of way, but in the way adults always tell teenagers they can't love. She knew it like she knew her name.

When he had finally, for the first time, come over to her house last year, she had giggled as he walked through the door—knowing the observation and judgment that was coming. Hers was a house of women—strong, independent, beautiful, Caribbean women. Three generations including her. Hues of assorted color, all with high cheekbones, upright carriage, and a constant banter of jokes and comments that filled the air, sometimes biting, but always love. A mother, who worked as a head nurse, survived all that came her way, had learned to expertly navigate a new and foreign land, always provided for her family, and saw everything as she judged quickly and permanently. An auntie, who had become Rastafarian, much to her own mother's disaproval, was an artist, seduced with a hug and an extra long beat of eye contact, and danced though life more than she walked. And a grandmother, who lived in her daughter's home and was thankful for her place in it, approved of her daughter's career as a nurse and the manner in which she ran the home and raised her granddaughter, but disapproved that her daughter did this raising alone, and of her choice in men, each and every one of them since her first, but she said little about this, except with her eyes, for her tone, was just like her—about as gentle as stone.

When Warrior had arrived at his friend's home, her mother was holding court while cooking a rich curry, potatoes peeking out, wooden spoon in her hand, permanently stained yellow from countless curries before this one, hair curly and tied back. She had welcomed him, her daughter's often discussed "friend" with a warm hug and searching eyes. She seemed to notice and like his strength immediately—his quiet confidence as well. In the caring way she looked at him she also seemd to notice his sadness. Her aunt immediately took his face in her hands and said his name with a Caribbean lilt, almost sang it, and then smiled and simply said, "Blessed." Her tiny grandmother looked up from her chair, her feet barely reaching the ottoman in front of her, peered over her glasses, and said, "So . . . ya me gran'dawta's frien'." It was not a question. As the assorted watchers watched Warrior, his "friend" ate her afternoon snack of bun and cheese, and when Warrior looked to her for help, she had laughed out loud through bites, her eyes letting him know he was safe to a degree—and entirely on his own. When he left, he realized that they had decided his future.

The cold was now cutting through their layers, and as they stood on the steps, he could feel that now she was thinking of his unique strength, but also how sad he was, even hopeless at times—he knew she was aware that he often woke up with rage. She looked scared. Scared to hold him. Scared not to. She took his hand.

Warrior looked through her eyes and saw within her. He saw how deeply she understood him. He knew she was also filled with pain, but he was uncomfortable that she seemed to be able to handle it so much better than he could—it didn't seem that it ever took her over, even for a minute. Her strength attracted him, and scared him too. She always seemed at peace. He struggled to keep looking her in the eye. He saw how desperately she always tried to clear the rage from his thoughts, to ease the flow of his blood. She was always with him, reminding him to breathe. And when he had seen too much, her spirit would brush his face, gently, claiming his eyes. He loved her for it—knew she could be like blood. Warrior knew this, he knew he should take her in his arms and let her ease the pain, but not today, today was different. His eyes were his, and they had just begun to see.

# CHAPTER 5

As Warrior moved through the streets of his neighborhood, he walked past the shrines without even glancing at their names, haunted by the memories of having been there when they were created. Where he lived, there were artists who specialized in the dead, their masterpieces morbid testimonies to those who had passed on. On many blocks blank walls of white brick were brightly spray-painted with images that told the tales of children who never had the chance to become grown.

Families, crews, and other loved ones would pay the graffiti men to perform their work. Then the artists would paint the image of the dead on the sides of abandoned buildings, creating tombstone portraits of fantasy configurations. Most would be dressed in finer clothes than they had ever worn, with more jewels than they had ever owned, standing in front of cars they had only driven in their dreams.

Other portraits reflected the grand possessions that deceased dealers had in fact owned in life, and the black or silver steel weapons they had used to get them—as they secured their short-lived glory. However, these shrines did not portray that without someone else's steel leading to their own death, their lives would never have been brought to the artist to paint. The images told of the dead's exploits in the trade of the white rock, but never the stories of those he had sent to the world to which he was just now arriving. Those who had been sent, victims whose stories ended before their time, innocent bystanders in the war of their generation, children whose lives weren't gone, yet they waited, anticipating the coming of their executioner, their young minds filled with the same simple question. "Why?" Whether they had sold it, used it, or simply been caught up in the war around it, all those who had passed on were remembered on the walls of names. Painted on the white brick, their different paths in life were woven together by the rock, like a braid. Behind the colorful image was always a tombstone, planted deeply in imaginary grass, sparkling in newness, filled with numbers and years of recent times, followed by the same three words: *Rest In Peace*. These are the walls that serve as the ledger for the steel, one-eyed god.

At the foot of the painted tombstones, on sidewalks which had served as the final bed before the fallen had passed on, the loved ones who were left maintained a vigil. Fulfilling the practices of long ago times, from a place only some still remembered as home, mutating the tradition for the urban landscape, they placed flowers, wreaths, burning candles and incense in makeshift altars, built in honor of the departed's name.

Cheap bottles of liquor, their contents consumed or poured out onto the earth called concrete, the glass bottles now serving as grave markers. The mourners placed these items down, knowing that by sunrise they would have to replace them again, for each night, the walking dead roamed the streets. These night walkers who were alive only in name, spent their time kneeling to the reign of the white rock. They would steal the silver fillings out of a sleeping man's mouth as he rested, and if he did not wake, would return for his ivory. They would take the flowers and wreaths as offerings to their god, and sell the candles for the few dollars that would ensure their return to their beloved and poisonous world. And if the walkers missed an altar, the weather would come, wind blowing away flowers, covering the streets with dirty petals, rains extinguishing candles, washing away chalk-written messages. This is a place where graveyards are found on every street, tombstones painted on brick walls. With so many dead, the space of tombstones are now overflowing, long lists of names flow down entire sides of buildings; but there is no shortage of graveyards in this land of the white rock.

Warrior crossed the street to the bodega to get something to drink. In front of the store, on top of a milk crate, sat Cowboy Johnson, a massive man with hard, calloused hands and an iron grip. He had been a rodeo star in the 1950s and it was rumored he had been one of the best cattle drivers the West had ever seen. He wore his worn brown leather cowboy boots, blue jeans with a leather belt that had a huge gold Texas lone star buckle, a thick canvas blue shirt, a silver and black cowboy string tie, and a five-gallon brown suede cowboy hat. In front of the corner store was Cowboy Johnson's spot, and he could always be found there, never drunk, but always slowly nursing his whiskey, holding court, telling the children stories about the Old West. As Warrior walked by, he nodded his head. Cowboy Johnson tipped his bottle of whiskey, covered in a brown paper bag, and nodded back.

Warrior walked into the back of the store where the cold drinks were kept. There were four sliding glass doors. Behind the first were juices and soda, behind the second was beer, and behind the other two were countless brands of malt liquor. In other neighborhoods, no malt liquor was sold due to its mind-altering strength and the large forty-ounce bottles it came in. In other neighborhoods, Warrior had not been able to find even one brand. In his neighborhood, the competition was so strong that the companies advertised everywhere; on the radio, on the billboards found on every street, rising high into the sky, and on signs glued to the windows of every corner bodega. In these stores, there was a different brand for every day of the week. Crazy Horse. St. Ides. Power. Dragon. Old E. Colt .45. The Bull. Different names. Same objective—to take the drinker into another world. Quick. Warrior reached behind the first glass door and took hold of a tall can of lemonade. His head pounded as visions of the day flooded his mind, and he put back the juice, sliding shut the door. He moved down the aisle, slid open another glass door, and wrapped his hand around the neck of a forty-ounce bottle of Crazy Horse. As he began to slide shut the glass door, Warrior once again felt the pounding in his head, and seeing the visions, and hearing the words, he reached back in, and grabbed another bottle. Warrior walked to the front of the store, placed the two bottles on the fake wood counter, and slid the cashier four dollars and fifty cents. The cashier put the two bottles into separate brown bags. Warrior placed them in the bag that hung from his shoulder, and walked out the door in the direction of the park.

As Warrior entered the park, he saw that much of the snow had melted since he had brought his sister there to play. Feet had trampled what remained underfoot, packing it down, turning it from a bright white to an off-gray. New garbage had been thrown to the ground, and wrappers, needles, plastic vials, and a few mud-soaked lost mittens, littered the earth as if the snow's cleaning job had been rebuffed by the city. Warrior felt a descending chill in the air, looked up at the skies and knew that nature's answer would soon come. Maybe tonight. Warrior walked deeper into the park, past where he and his sister had built their snowman, long since destroyed, and looked for a bench. He was in a desolate area, and Warrior was happy for the peace. Then he heard Weatherman.

"Hey! Young brutha! Hey!"

Warrior stopped walking and turned in the direction of the voice. Weatherman was standing in the snow, sweating. His umbrella was hanging from his exhausted arm, its point wet with snow and mud. Warrior knew that Weatherman had been mastering his thrusts, perfecting his samurai strokes, for hours, probably all day. He was preparing for battle. Weatherman could wield his umbrella with vengeance. In fact, one night Warrior had seen him fighting off some young boys who had been acting foolish. They had tried to mess with Weatherman as he slept, and he had woken, unsheathed his umbrella, and taken to teaching those boys a lesson. Not hurting them mind you, just teaching. Warrior had laughed as Weatherman chased the boys, sticking them in their ass cheeks with the point of the umbrella, expertly smacking them in their backs with its broad side, paying no mind to their swearing that they would never bother him again. Weatherman brought up his umbrella and pointed it at Warrior.

"You, young brutha, I'm talkin' to you!" he said, slightly out of breath.

"What's up, man?" Warrior asked.

"The sky. And what's up with you?" replied Weatherman.

"I'm jus' tryin' to find a place to sit down. I thought I'd be able to have a little peace in here, you know? Away from the noise," said Warrior.

"There's lots a peace to be found in the park. Trees. Ponds. Animals. Birds. Mother Nature brings peace," Weatherman said, waving his umbrella all around him. "Ya figured out who stole the sun?" Weatherman said, his head leaning to one side, as he peered at Warrior.

"No," Warrior replied softly as he slowly shook his head and turned, walking deeper into the park. Weatherman's voice followed after him.

"The wind is callin' out, young brutha. Put your ear to the air, you can hear it. The wind's got voice. Can't ya hear it cryin'? Even the wind wants to be free . . ."

Weatherman's voice faded away as Warrior walked into a heavily wooded section of the park. He walked for a while and then broke through the dense trees, into a clearing, seeing a pond surrounded by a path that wove around the water's edge. Warrior walked down the sloped hill that lay between him and the pond, and sat down on one of the green wood benches that lined the winding path. He removed one of the bottles of Crazy Horse from his bag, keeping it within its brown paper confines. As Warrior tapped the bottle in the way he had been taught, he felt the temperature dropping and knew that the alcohol would keep him warm. He broke the seal of the bottle, threw away the cap, and turned the bottle to its side, pouring out some of its contents. This was custom. Some call it libation. Some call it paying respect. Whatever the name, it means honoring those who are not here, and those who are locked up. Before you drink, you acknowledge the voices who have passed on. Ancestors. Elders. Children. This is the law.

Warrior brought the bottle to his mouth, closed his eyes, and drank deeply. Immediately the alcohol flooded his head, running through his blood, bringing warmth and heavy eyes. He sat there, cradling the neck of the bottle, looking out at the pond. Its dark waters were covered with a thin layer of ice, and in some spots the water had broken through. He placed his earphones on, took his music player out of his pocket, chose the soundtrack for the mood, and pulled his hood up tightly, keeping the warmth in and disturbing sounds outside. He pressed play and let the sounds and the malt liquor take him into another world.

It was dark now. Snow had begun to fall almost an hour before. Whiteness covered the iced layer of the pond, and returned purity to the park. Streetlamps lined the path around the pond, but only one was working, its light straining to erase the shadows. The bench Warrior sat on was far from the rays of the light so he sat in darkness, the dim glow of the moon reflecting slightly off his black hood and black jacket, snow falling around him, flakes building up on his still shoulders. The only part of his body that moved was his head. It nodded, continuously, following the rhythm of the drumbeat. One bottle lay discarded at his feet, another, almost empty, rested in his lap, his hand gently maintaining its balance. Warrior's jaw tightened, and his lips mouthed the words that flowed through his ears, their sounds long ago memorized. Warrior's head kept time as he looked out through hooded bloodshot eyes.

The voices of genocide and ignorance had been calling Warrior's name, trying to reach him, but this night, he was not listening. He felt the rage flowing through his veins, and it felt good. It brought warmth, and clarity to his thoughts.

*These are words that would make Harriet Tubman smile. These are words that would ring true in the ears of Malcolm. These are words that Nat Turner used in Virginia, in 1831. These are our words. Martin spoke of another way. He preached, "Mine eyes have seen the glory of the comin' of the Lawd." Well, mine eyes have never seen such a thing. Why? I walk, following the sounds of the voices and the footprints of the spirits. Mine eyes have seen a jungle, and in this jungle, I am the hunted, hunting the hunter. I am the turner of tides. They say that hatred is destructive, that it poisons the blood. But they fail to see that it gives us earth in which to cast down our roots, polluted as it may be. Like my grandmamma always said: Two wrongs might not make a right, but they damn sure make things even.*

*It's time for an eye for an eye. A life for a life. Time to go back to Old Times. We've been turning the other cheek for too long, and we dying because of it. While we sit around the table, trying to get them to hear us, it is our blood that's spilling, not theirs. Why? Our blood demands that times change. So if we must die, then these, will be dying times. My eyes have seen much pain. They've seen much death. Now they see retribution in the air. A wise elder once said, "It is no more harm for you to kill a man who is tryin' to kill you, than it is to take a drink of water, when thirsty." Well, we're thirsty, we've been thirsty. And water can't quench it. I say no more water. It's been told that "God gave Noah the rainbow sign, No more water, the fire next time." Well I've heard the voices, and I've seen the signs, and they say, the fire this time. The fire this time.*

Warrior heard the response. The voices chanted for fire. This time, they would answer his call.

Warrior stood and swallowed the last of his liquor. He dropped the bottle to the ground and walked up the sloping hill that led from the benches to the densely wooded area of trees. The trees served as a border, separating the pond from the more open sections of the park. As he walked toward this border, Warrior looked down and saw tracks leading into the wooded area. He followed their path, leaving the dim light of the pond for the absolute darkness of the trees. This was one of the areas that most in the city avoided, afraid of desperate people in desperate times. Warrior liked the desolation, and he had no fear of such people. The desperate dead were another story.

As he followed the tracks deeper into the darkness, Warrior imagined what the stray dog that must have left them had looked like. He imagined its drooping skin, its protruding ribs.

Most likely it had smelled food in the woods, or maybe it was seeking some protection from the snow. The newly fallen flakes crunched under Warrior's boots as he walked, still following the tracks, the clearest path in the darkness. Warrior studied them as he walked, and wondered at the great number of tracks that had been left. Maybe it was a pack of dogs, or . . . wolves. Just as Warrior stopped moving, a strong blow came to his chest and he was thrown down into the snow. There was darkness all around him. The claw held him firmly in place.

*Didn't hear the wolves, did you?*

*No. Where are they?*

*With their master.*

*And where is genocide this night?*

*Just passed by. Was watching you for a while. Appreciated the vision. Then moved on. The wolves followed. Why? Is my grip not enough to hold you?*

*Ignorance is enough to hold anyone. Like a cage.*

*Had something to drink I see. Head a little clouded, thoughts blurred?*

Warrior heard the laugh form.

*Why do you not come with us Warrior? Let us show you the riches that could be yours. It's so easy. You could stop running. Stop fighting. Stop struggling. Just walk our path.*

*Never. It is the path that leads to nowhere.*

*It leads to our Gods.*

*I don't bow to your gods. Your money does not seduce me.*

*Everyone bows.*

The claw tightened its grip, pressing Warrior deeper into the snow.

*Not me . . .*

The claw spoke softly now. *Everyone, by time's end, kneels to our Gods' reign. Why do you think you have the strength to resist their alluring call, the seduction?*

*My religion forbids it. And the voices are too strong, even for you demons.*

*And these voices, their names are?*

*I would die before I would tell you.*

*As you wish,* the claw said as it released Warrior. *As you wish . . .*

Warrior lay on his back in the darkness as the rhythm of his breathing returned to normal. The snowfall was heavier now than it had been when he was sitting by the pond. It covered his body. The sky filled with angry, swirling clouds warned that its wrath was just beginning. Warrior stared up and thought about what he had just done.

There are those who choose to make peace with their demons. They swear never to confront them, nor to seek to evade them, resigned to allow fate to run its course. There are others who make deals with their demons. They walk to the Crossroads, sell their souls, ensuring that they will never be haunted in this life while possessing their dreams as they walk the earth. For this, they know their souls will one day belong to the demons, knowing nothing but nightmares in the next world. There are those who simply turn and run, believing that they can escape their demons with swiftness of foot. The demons know better. For if their hellhounds do not return those who flee, time will. No one can run forever. And then there are those who feel they have the power to walk the path. They believe they can stare the demons in their eyes and make them blink. Almost always, these stares are met with howling laughter as the demons devour their souls. But those who do survive this meeting of eyes fill the myths and the legends of history. Their stories are passed down for generations, defeating time. Warrior had chosen this path of legion. He had declared war on his demons.

Breathing deeply, he closed and opened his eyes, trying to clear his head of the effects of the Crazy Horse and the ringing sound of the claw. He shook his head slowly, pulled himself up and stood, the alcohol making him dizzy. He gathered himself and walked out of the wooded area.

The park was empty as Warrior made his way through the snow toward the city streets. The wind was howling, and everyone was inside, finding shelter. The birds, squirrels, raccoons, rats, and other small animals that called the park home were hidden, too. They found protection within the deep branches of trees, the carved-out holes of trunks, underneath the earth and snow, beneath the ground in the city sewers. This night was no time for life. As Warrior moved toward the stone arches at the edge of the park, he passed the spot where he had seen Weatherman earlier. Even Weatherman was gone.

As the snow began to fall heavily, and the wind howled tasting the chill in the air, Warrior imagined Weatherman had also seen rage in the sky. Most likely he had used his umbrella to clear a path in search of the warmth of one of the hidden caves that only he knew of—caves in the deepest bowels of the park, hidden from ordinary eyes who did not know the park held such things. If the walk to the caves was too far on a night like this, Weatherman would have found warmth within one of the park's many dark, damp tunnels. On this night, the wind would not speak with comforting words even to Weatherman, but instead would shriek his name.

Warrior reached his building and as he entered felt the sudden rush of heat, the result of the tireless work of radiators pumping heat into the once chilled air. As he reached his floor, he walked right past his door, continuing up the flights of stairs to the fourth floor, then the fifth, and then the sixth. Reaching the final floor of apartments, Warrior walked down the long hallway where a flickering light showed the way toward the flight of stairs that led up to the roof. As he made his way up the darkened staircase, he had begun to sweat from the sudden change in temperature, from the exertion, and from the heat trapped close to his body, captured by the layers of clothes he wore. As the beads of perspiration trickled down his back, he stood at the roof's door, slid open the two, steel, bolt locks, placed his hand on the dark green door, its paint long ago peeled by moisture, and pushed. He used all of his strength, forcing it open, the pressure of the wind blowing violently against the metal of the door.

Warrior stood on the edge of the roof of his building, looking down at the city, his feet firmly planted on top of the cold stone brick of the three-foot wall that surrounded the circumference of the roof.

The snow swirled around Warrior's head, whiteness covered everything, reaching the windows of the cars. The street lamps cast a yellow hue on the whiteness, and the moon glowed silver.

It had become a blizzard, and Warrior stood in the eye of the storm. He stared ahead at the dense dark sky, the color of blue that folks down South call blurple, and he listened to the fury of the wind. The storm had wiped the streets clean, its mighty, intimidating power staking claim to the night. But Warrior shared in this claim—sought no shelter from nature's wrath. He wished he could be even closer though, to stand in the clouds, letting the force run through him, stealing some of its power. Warrior continued to look to the sky, and remembered what it felt like to fly.

When Warrior was young, he had always dreamed of flying. Whenever troubles had become too great, whenever the pain was too much to bear, Warrior had simply taken to the air and flown. When bullies filled the streets, when the cutting laughter of other children had sliced too deeply, when he had gotten into trouble and he knew he would have to face the looks of his father and the words of his mother, he flew. When he had felt the breath of the monsters on his neck, when the cries of the voices rang in his mind, following him everywhere, he had taken to the air and flown. Warrior always knew there was no trouble too great, no pain that could break him, for if the dreams became too much, he could fly away.

He would soar through the air, gliding, searching, like a hawk. He flew over massive, snowcapped mountain ranges, through dark forests that otherwise would have scared him, over waterfalls, looking down as he glided over the red earth of the Georgia soil, flying all the way to the mighty ocean. In the air he would find peace, quiet, and solitude, away from the drums of others. He would hover above the breaking waves of the ocean, the blue-green water pounding the shores, its power crushing rock into sand. Entranced, Warrior would look down, hearing the repeated pounding, the beating of the water, endlessly keeping time.

He would never continue on his path to fly out over the ocean, because he couldn't remember the way across the water. It was unknown to him, the path forgotten long ago. Hearing the rhythm of the waves, he would hear voices calling out his name, not Warrior, not even his birth name, but another one he knew was his. He heard a tongue that he could not understand, but somewhere deep inside of him knew he had once spoken. The voices sang, trying to make him remember those familiar words, now forgotten. The wild waters would crash down, and the words would be lost in the roar. Warrior would look out into the distance, trying to hear through his confusion. He knew, somewhere in his soul, in his memory, that the voices were blood, that he had heard their sounds before, sometime, somewhere that he should have answered their call. Eventually he would turn away, resigned, deciding that the words were just another haunting voice he did not understand. Gathering the air under him, he would flap his wings twice and glide with hawk's speed back home.

Now, as he stood on the edge of the roof, convinced that he could fly, he could barely see. The raging blizzard blowing snow into his eyes blinded him. As the thoughts of his childhood dreams filled his mind, Warrior heard the quiet scream that served as the song, foretelling the arrival of the one with no name. The claw had visited him earlier, now it was another demon's turn. Warrior remembered its call like that of an old friend. As the sound filled his mind, he felt the heat of the wolves' breath, their jaws biting at his heels, their lips pulled back over razor-sharp teeth as they growled in fury . . .

*Flying would bring so much freedom . . . Would it not, Warrior? Imagine the power you would possess. Imagine what you could see.*

Then it whispered:

*You would be able to travel the seven seas by night, and the seven lands by day. The world would hold no secrets from you. Your name would be sung by all peoples. Warrior: the Traveler, the Seer, the Wise Man of the Earth. Nothing would be outside your reach.*

The seductive, hushed tones encircled Warrior's head, possessing his ears so that he heard nothing else, not even the sound of the wolves.

*You could release the chains, be free from the voices, and go to a place where there are no wolves, there would be no pain, you could just fly, and it would not follow.*

Warrior could feel the words brushing against his ears. Their tantalizing sound caused his knees to bend, his toes curling through his boots extending over the roof's edge, his legs tensing as his body prepared to take to the air. Warrior's eyes were blinded by the storm, his thoughts clouded by the Crazy Horse. His head was pounding furiously as the wind howled around him and the teeth of the wolves snapped at his feet, driving him from the edge. The winds pushed and pulled as Warrior's body leaned over the edge of the building, his arms preparing to become wings. The air felt strong, so if his first attempts were shaky, like the steps of a newborn foal, the air would steady him, cradling him, until his wings felt sturdy enough to fly.

*Yes. The wind will blow like the gentle hand of a mother. They will not allow you to fall. The winds will show you the way. Listen to my song and fly, Warrior. Fly. Fly, fly away . . .*

It was wrong. It had made a mistake, and suddenly Warrior knew it. Faith crept, forcefully, into his thoughts. He saw his mother's face. He heard his father's words. He felt his sister's hand inside of his. The voices spoke, shattering the silence.

His thoughts jarred, Warrior's body hovered now, leaning over the roof's edge as the wind swirled furiously around him and the snarling wolves bit the air, inches from his feet. Warrior relaxed his legs, uncurled his toes, and fought the swaying of his body. As his feet struggled to remain planted on the stone wall of the roof, the sneering words surrounded him.

*You will join your brethren now. Another "soldier" falls on the battlefields. Another boy fills my ranks, so much easier to control than a man. It is truly getting too easy now. Even the leaders fall. I used to have to chase your kin, now they come to me, blind fools who believe that I am their destiny. Your dead kindred await you at the graveyard, Warrior. Welcome.*

Warrior remembered blood and became angry. It was not his time. His brethren would have to wait. He was not yet finished serving as witness. He called on the voices and the wolves disappeared, the scream fell silent. Warrior leaned back into the howling wind, straining to steady himself, and then he planted his feet firmly on the brick wall. His balance restored, Warrior tilted his head back and acknowledged the sky. Then, he exhaled deeply and stepped down.

The roof was empty. There were no wolves, no voices, and the demon had moved on. Warrior stood in the middle of the blizzard, the snow now reaching above his knees. He moved through the snowdrifts, some blown up against the chimney and the water tank now sloped up past Warrior's head. He reached the roof door and, gripping the handle, prepared himself for the struggle of opening it against the piled up snow. But as he pulled, he found that it opened with surprising ease. The wind had suddenly changed direction, and its gusts aided Warrior in forcing the movement of the creaking door. He walked through the opened space, turned around to close the door, and one last time looked out into the blinding storm.

As the snow blew into the stairwell, its drift flowing through the door, Warrior felt the freezing wind against his face. He looked at the colors of the night—black, purple, silver, and the white that poured from within the darkness—as he observed the colorful sky, his mind questioned but paid silent respect to the power, the intimidating beauty. Afraid of the answers the night's sky might reveal, he lowered his eyes and closed the door.

In his room, he took his jacket off and hung it in the closet, then turned on the radio. He needed to hear music, to hear other voices that did not seek to speak to him. The station was playing one of his favorite songs, and as he slowly began to undress shedding his wet clothes, Warrior listened. Exhausted, he sat on the edge of his bed, absently untying the laces of his boots. He kicked them off and fell back onto the bed, his chest bare. As he lay there, calming his thoughts, his song ended, and the DJ began to speak, her voice melting seductively through the air, caressing Warrior's ears.

Suddenly, from the radio came the sound of a high-pitched noise, announcing a special news report. The official-sounding voice began to speak, its loud and enunciated words grated on Warrior's ears, contrasting with the sensual, smooth flow of the DJ's voice.

> *"This is a special news bulletin: There has been a snow day announced for all city schools tomorrow. All elementary. All junior high. And all high schools. Will be closed. I repeat. There will be no schools open tomorrow. All city schools have been canceled . . ."*

Warrior sat up from his bed, leaned over to the radio and turned off the alarm set for the morning. Now he would not have to get up early in the cold darkness. He stood up and removed what was left of his clothes. He placed them over the back of his chair, turned off his light, and climbed into bed naked. He pulled the covers up around his shoulders and lay wrapped inside the blankets, looking at the frost on his window. The icy layer distorted the glass, making it impossible to see outside. The faintest rays of light from the streetlamps seeped through the window, creating a thick, stained glass effect. The glass played tricks on Warrior's eyes, making him see imagined designs caused by the frost. His eyes became heavy, unable to focus on the window art. His ears took over, and then he heard the voices as he fell deeply into sleep. Warrior no longer strained to see faces full of pain. He was content to hear his own cries.

*I lay in the dark, damp hull of a two-hundred-ton ship. The boat swayed back and forth, side to side, as if it moved to the memory of the beating of the drum. I could not sit. I could not stand. I could not rise. I was shackled, hand and foot, to the man next to me. The hull stank of shit, blood, and death. This was the passage to the unknown. The sharks that swam next to the boat were the hellhounds who served as guides, ensuring that we were following the marked trail of human skeletons that lay beneath us. A child died, and I slept. The nightmare descended.*

*A man appeared. A Black man. A Negro. A Nigger. He was tall, and he wore long, tattered overalls, and a burlap potato sack as a shirt. He wore no shoes, and his feet were hard. His face was like worn leather, and his eyes . . . cold. They were the color of ebony, and they were set deeply into the blue-black skin of his face. They screamed of pain, and warned of the retribution carried in his heart. They told the tale of a man who had seen, and was more deadly for his visions.*

*He removed the burlap sack, let down the straps of his overalls, allowing them to hang from his waist, and then he turned his back to me. It was something I had never seen. My worst nightmares* had not brought forth such sights. The dark skin of his back looked as if an animal had clawed it to pieces in a rage. It was inhuman. His back spoke of where the path of human skeletons led. His back spoke of the unknown. The scars were the words of his warning. The words said:

I stand witness
To the treachery
Here is my testimony
Listen to my word:
Good morning Slave.

Your nightmares
Are your most pleasant dreams
Your curses,
Words to be whispered in a lover's ear
I am the signature,
Announcing flesh that is owned
The blood that ran,
Carried memory
The scars that came,
History
I serve as proof
That freedom is just a word
Your destiny,
Has been entrenched on your back

Hello Slave.

*Your existence began in chains,*
*And so it will end*

*Good night Slave . . .*

I opened my eyes, remembering ebony eyes that sang of a reckoning, and waited for my new name.

# CHAPTER 6

Wolves were the sound of the wind. It was all that Warrior could hear. That, and the drums. The speaker's hands beat them, slowly, forcefully, announcing an arrival. The ceremony had begun.

As Warrior had lain in bed, the bright sun had shone through his window waking him, the brightness making him squint in its glare. His mother and sister had left the house hours before he had awakened, on one of their adventures created to fill the school snow day. Warrior knew they were either walking the galleries of a museum or gliding around the ice skating rink in the middle of the park. Whatever it was, he had missed out on the adventure, having slept off the effects of the Crazy Horse.

It was past mid-day. He got out of bed and took a long, hot shower. He got dressed, in black. Black boots. Black jeans.

Black sweatshirt. Black leather jacket. Black skullcap. The day called for black. It felt good on his skin.

He locked all of the locks and walked down the stairs. He wanted to see the aftermath of the storm, to see what remained in its wake. As he left his building and he felt the snow still falling, he smiled. Nature had not yet finished answering. The flakes dropped gently against his face. They were light, as if they drifted with no force. The storm had fought hard, but it had lost the great battle, and now its flakes were melting before they reached the ground. The snow that had accumulated during the night was piled high, reaching to Warrior's waist, testimony to the great struggle waged under the glow of the moon. But even the fury with which the snow had fallen could not prevent the coming of whatever it was that nature had fought. Surrounded by the sound of the wolves and the beating of the drums, Warrior could feel its presence.

By late afternoon, he stood in the belly of the beast, a beast whose innards are filled with the chaos that is its nourishment. There was snow everywhere; no stores were open, and the traffic lights swayed, many of their bulbs broken, the wind having won at least that battle. Within this silence, bedlam ruled the streets.

But the blue soldiers were everywhere. They ran, wearing helmets with long visors that covered their throats, carrying clear, bulletproof shields, their batons raised high to the sky. There was the deafening sound of sirens, of glass breaking, and voices shouting. Blue and red lights flashed, their swirling colors filling eyes, as the blue soldiers' cars were the only ones that moved through the streets, their tires spitting snow as they turned. The soldiers ran frantically, trying to repair the invisible walls that had been broken. These walls had taken centuries to build; the mortar was hard, but the brick brittle. It had taken only the morning to bring them down.

*But as we speak, the masons are coming.*

Word on the street was that it happened early that morning. The blue soldiers had shot a boy, and finally folks decided it was time. Nobody bothered to ask what time it was, it was just . . . time. Warrior looked out at the commotion as he walked among crumbling walls, and thought of other walls.

*We break down these walls so that they can see what has been done to us, but what we don't seem to understand is that they know the world being lived within these walls better than we do ourselves, because they created them. Bringing down the walls doesn't change the lives being lived inside of 'em, it only brings the sight of the lives to those who are blind. Walk the streets with me, see what I see, and tell me what has changed. Salvation won't come from outside these walls, it will come from within. The sound you hear is the laughter of demons. They relish the fact that we have not learned. That we still believe that if we cry loud enough, that the creators of the walls will hear us, and show us the way out. The demons laugh, knowing that only we can bring about our deliverance from their hell. And instead of attacking the demons, we waste our time on walls.*

As Warrior turned the corner, he saw two young boys running, narrowly evading the swinging batons of four blue soldiers.

The batons were getting closer. The boys were out of breath, and though fear drove their weary legs through the snow, they would soon falter and fall into the hands of the soldiers. Warrior continued walking as the speaker's hands began to sweat, the drums beating faster.

As Warrior moved through the tense streets, he saw that at least one business in the neighborhood was continuing as usual. In an alley that ran between two high buildings, one of the walking dead was doing business with a shadow. It was a normal sight, one that Warrior had seen almost every day of his life, except this time, standing next to the woman who bartered with the shadow, was a little girl. The girl's dress blew in the wind, her worn spring jacket offering no protection from the biting cold, and so she pressed her body against her mother, seeking warmth. Warrior stood at the opening of the alley, looking at the scene.

The woman could have been pitied. She was thin. Bone thin. Her body was withered and had no shape. Where her high, round ass had once met thick thighs, there was now nothing but a long, narrow back. Her bones seemed fragile, delicate and dry, as if a strong breeze might crack them. Her wrists were too weak to hold her hands straight, so they dangled limply in the air. She moved as if she had been broken, and having just recently been glued back together was now afraid that any sudden movement might shatter her all over again. Maybe it was in the way that she hunched her shoulders, or the way she walked, keeping her legs pressed tightly together, shuffling her feet in old, tattered plastic boots. She walked like a child, with her arms folded protectively across her chest, embracing her body. Her head was too big for her gaunt neck, and the neck bent forward from the strain of attempting to keep her head high. And so she no longer fought the strain, and allowed it to hang.

Her skin was dry and ashy. Her polyester clothes sagged from her shriveled body as if she were a little girl playing dress-up with her mother's clothes. Her once permed hair was now unkempt, her feeble attempts at straightening it had made large patches fall out, and so she covered the ragged mess with a filthy bandanna. It was in her face that one could read the tale of the path she walked. Her cheeks were sunken, emphasizing the stark outline of her jaw. The sharp jawline came together in lips painted with a shade of lipstick that was too red, more fitting for a clown than a woman. Above that painted smile were hollow, haunted eyes that rested in deep, darkened sockets. Her mind struggled to remember the beauty secrets, those taught to her as a young girl. Her body tried to move in the way that had once been instinct, the natural swaying of her wide hips bringing crooked smiles to men's faces. Now her sight only brought laughter. She had knelt too many times in order to get the rock for anyone to remember who she had once been. Her faded beauty lived only in her mind.

The woman now stood in an alley. Her small daughter faced the opposite direction, one arm wrapped around her mother's leg, one hand raised, her extended thumb dangling from her lower lip. The girl's eyes stared down, and if she still had a spirit that she claimed, it was in hiding. The girl was silent as her mother spoke. The woman had no money, and so she offered the shadow anything for some of the rock. He told her that she was dried up, and that even shadows hear rumors. She offered anything again, this time with her daughter. The shadow handed the woman the rock, removed the small, clutching hand off the woman's leg, and led the girl into the darkness. The drums beat faster.

As the figures disappeared into the shadows, Warrior felt heat on the back of his neck and turned around to look into blazing flames. A small four-story stone apartment building between a liquor store and a church was burning. The fiery, red-orange color that engulfed the structure and poured out through its windows shone in contrast to the whiteness that surrounded it. The snow that fell from the broken roof into the fire did nothing to hinder the flames. And in the moments that Warrior watched, the raging fire overtook the slight resistance of the ice-covered stone and consumed the entire building. As the firemen rode up in their truck, arriving to ensure the flames did not spread to the adjoining buildings, Warrior saw that the alley he had been looking into remained untouched by fire. The heat was powerful, and even from a distance it singed Warrior's face. With the arrival of the firemen, too many blue soldiers had come, and so Warrior moved away from the heat.

As he walked, Warrior realized that the overwhelmed soldiers were depending on the freezing cold to aid them in clearing the streets. The weather was brutal, and as the sun began to descend, the temperature dropped even further, and many of the people who had been out all day started to make their way home. These crowds had stood on sidewalks, watching the action, observing the rage, wanting to keep a safe distance from the fires. They had not thrown one stone, or screamed one word, they had not even had the desire nor the strength to walk among those who revolted. They were content to simply stand at a safe distance and pass judgment. They hadn't felt the blinding anger run through their blood, they hadn't been burned by the heat of the flames, or been chased by the blue soldiers. They hadn't had to run from swinging batons. They hadn't heard the wolves howling all day.

But above the call of the voices, in a different realm from the shrieks of the sirens, the explosion of gunshots, and the breaking of glass, Warrior had heard the wolves. They had kept him company, their familiar sound walking with him as he moved throughout the streets. Warrior had listened differently on this day. He had tried to take himself within their sound. He had tried to enter the world of the wolves, to speak their language, to join their pack. It was no longer enough to hear their sound; he had to know what it was that they sought, what drove them. Warrior walked along the streets, looking down at the pavement, listening to the wolves. When he finally brought his eyes up from the ground, Warrior saw Weatherman.

Weatherman was outside of the park, and that was something Warrior had never seen. He stood in the middle of the block on the front steps of an abandoned building, mumbling. He held his umbrella in both hands, pointing it up at the setting sun. His head was twitching, but the rest of his body was rigid. The umbrella did not waver, its steadiness remaining true. As Warrior moved closer to Weatherman, he heard that the words were being spoken softly, their muffled sound escaping through Weatherman's tightened jaw. Weatherman's eyes stared straight ahead.

"The wind speaks, an' no one listens. The rains scream, an' no one hears. Lightnin' brings light to blind eyes. Thunder sound to deaf ears. Nature teaches, but don't nobody follow Her Word. I hear Her Word, She's my God. And your Gods are?

"Your fire is here. So what has it brought? Open your eyes, it's seein' times, and seein' always teaches more than bein' sold. 'Cause now, we don't even own our eyes. We see through eyes transplanted through centuries, filled with visions of the wrong damn times. So what do we do with a lost people? A wanderin' tribe that no longer knows the way? The bones know. Ask the bones. Wanna know pain? Imagine dyin' in the spirit world. We need our eyes back. But since we ain't got time to wait, maybe we can reach 'em through voice. Maybe they can hear their way to freedom. It's a long path away from the beast, gotta have a guide. Time to go to the Blood Council and ask 'em for a voice to reach the wanderin' ones . . . Yeah, that'll do. Listen now, 'cause the Word only comes once:

"Bruthas and Sistahs . . .
I come to you this evenin', to talk about a
    Dragon.
Yes, I said a Dragon.

Bruthas and Sistahs . . .
I also come to you this evenin', to talk about a
    boy.
But ya see, the story I have to tell you this
    evenin', don't begin with no Dragon.
And it don't begin with no boy.
This story, begins with a woman.

What her name was is not important, what is
   important, is that you know she was strong.
Now when this woman was large with child,
   when she carried a life inside a her womb,
   she engaged in a battle that shook the very
   foundation of this world.
I say the very foundation.
This child that breathed inside a her was her
   firstborn—not the Seventh Son, but the
   First.
And when she became heavy with this child,
   when it came time for her to bear,
the Heavens began to swirl.
Lightnin' broke 'cross the sky.
Thunder pounded the Earth.
And the ground became restless.
And then, what had been foretold came to pass:
the Dragon reared its head.
The Scripture reads:
'And the dragon stood before the woman
   which was ready to be delivered for to
   devour her child as soon as it was born . . .'
This Dragon would not even give her child the
   chance of life.
The Dragon lay by the woman's sweatin' and
   strainin' body, waitin', seekin' to make her
   child his meal.
And from her womb, this woman brought
   forth a man-child.

And we are told that when this manchild was
   born, the woman was given the wings of
   a great eagle so that she might soar to the wilderness, and away from the jaws of the beast.
And in this bosom she would be nourished,
and her child would be nourished, for time,
   and time, and half a time.
Here, in the wilderness, she would be free
   from the face of the Dragon.
And when the Dragon came to realize that
   the woman had escaped from its clutches,
   that the fate it had destined for the woman's
   young child had been evaded, the Dragon
   was filled with a fury that could not be
   contained.
And it shook the Earth.
And so this Dragon called forth its demons,
   and there was war in the wilderness.
The woman and the angels fought.
And the Dragon and its demons fought.
And there was war in the wilderness.
War.
And when the Dragon and its kin seemed too
   strong, when the wrath of the beast seemed
   too mighty, the woman and the angels
   fought harder.
And it is here that the Scripture teaches us:
   'And they overcame the dragon by the
   blood, and by the word of their testimony.'

I said, by the Blood,
and by the Word of their Testimony.
And when the Dragon saw that it was
    defeated, rage rolled down.
The Book tells us: 'And the dragon was wroth
    with the woman, and went to make war
    with the remnant of her seed . . .'
The Dragon could not defeat the mother, so it
    sought out the child.
But what the Dragon failed to see, what was
    its fatal mistake, was that this man-child
    carried the same blood in his veins as that
    of his mother, and his life had come to pass
    hearin' the word of her testimony.
The Dragon sought to make war with the seed,
    but others stood with it.
The seed carried the Blood, knew the Word,
    and had heard the Testimony. He would not
    stand alone.
That is why he is known as the man-child.
That is why we tell his story.
That is why we spread the Word.

And so it has been said . . ."


    As Weatherman finished speaking, his body swayed, resting limply against the side of the stone stoop that led up to the boarded-up building. Then he lifted his bowed head and turned in the direction of Warrior.

"Imagine that. Weatherman gettin' the spirit. Ain't that somethin'? Guess the Council workin' in mysterious ways these days," Weatherman said, slowly shaking his head as his voice calmed, regaining its whisper. He moved down the steps of the stoop, his umbrella leading the way, his hushed voice once again carrying on about the weather. He walked down the street, carefully making his way back to the park, to the protection of his true God.

Warrior stood at the foot of the stoop, watching Weatherman walk away. Weatherman's words had joined the cries of the wolves and the beating of the drum, and now Warrior's mind was pulsing, full of sounds and voices. The wolves were shrieking louder than Warrior had ever heard them, their call almost sounding human, tormented souls finally on the heels of their redemption.

Blue soldiers sped by, their car sirens blasting. Bottles were thrown, glass shattered, and somewhere close by, gunshots rang out. Warrior looked down the street and saw that the soldiers were running, trying to find the shooter. The street was deserted, and so Warrior quickly ran up the steps. The door of the building was boarded up with thick plywood and chained shut, but the wood that covered one of the windows on the ground floor had been destroyed by the storm. A few thick splinters of frozen wood still hung from the top of the window. Warrior kicked them in and stepped through the building. The drums were pounding now, the speaker's hand beating them, urgently.

The room was damp, it stank of urine and burnt charcoal-scarred wood. A thick layer of crushed brick covered the floor. On top of this layer were the littered remnants of broken needles and empty glass vials. There was a sound of crunching as Warrior moved through the room. From the ceiling, a loose light socket hung from its frayed cord; Warrior saw discarded clothes and a soiled mattress, remnants of someone's home. The stench of the place made Warrior dizzy, and he moved toward the back of the building to another room.

This room was even darker, but it had cleaner air. It had not been used so often, and it smelled musty, like a house sealed for too long. Warrior stumbled against a pile of dry bricks and broken wood that lay in the center of the room, and he sat down on the pile, surrounded by darkness.

As he rested, Warrior could still hear the faint sounds of the sirens, their hum seeping through the cracks in the old building. He could also hear voices coming from the roof— they sounded like screams, but by now he couldn't tell anymore. As most of the sounds from the outside melted away, the wolves and the beating of the drums remained, and Warrior sat there, listening.

It was some time later when Warrior felt the hand. At first it just rested on his shoulder, but then, as Warrior turned violently drawing back, it reached out and gently touched his face. Warrior brought his head back, but the hand remained. Warrior could now feel the hand was that of a child. It was so small. The tiny fingers were soft as a baby's skin, and they caressed Warrior's features, touching, sensing, remembering. The fingers sought answers. They brushed across Warrior's eyes, his nose, his lips, as if the face belonged to the hand. The fingers knew every rise, every depression.

The child then took Warrior's hand and spread his fingers, making Warrior touch the unseen face. Warrior could only tell that the face belonged to a small boy. His fingers glided over the fat baby cheeks and the broad, wide nose. His hand felt the head of the child and found that no hair grew there, only the faintest feel of stubble, the smoothness of a head shaved repeatedly. He could feel the child's pulse beating and was surprised that it beat so slow. In the darkness, surrounded by blue soldiers and the sounds, Warrior's heart beat fast, but here, in this place, the boy's pulse beat as slow as time moves on a blistering Southern day. The boy took Warrior's hand from his head and brought Warrior's fingers down to his opened eyelids. Warrior tried to bring back his hand, not wanting to injure the child's eyes, but before he could, Warrior's own eyes closed in recognition. The child had no eyes.

The boy took Warrior's hand and led him out of the dark room. They walked toward the dimly lit staircase that rose up from the floor at the center of the building. The storm window up on the roof had long ago been shattered, and the light of dusk shone down, illuminating the stairwell with gray hues. As they climbed the rickety staircase, the boy leading, Warrior following, the voices on the roof became clearer, and Warrior knew they were screams. The boy's hand gripped two of Warrior's fingers tightly, leading Warrior up the stairs toward the voices. The staircase was made of wood and had been eaten away by years of erosion. As the boy held on to Warrior, Warrior felt for the first time that the boy was pressing—whatever lay at the top of the stairs was important, and the boy was insistent that Warrior follow. He allowed the boy to lead him, content to see what lay ahead, moving to the urgent call of the drums.

Out on the roof, Warrior's eyes scanned the tops of the nearby buildings and looked up into the sky, becoming accustomed to the dull light that surrounded him. It was the kind of light found toward the end of dusk, right before nightfall. The kind of light that offered plenty of hiding places for shadows. The roof seemed empty, but Warrior noticed deep tracks in the snow; men had walked here and had dragged someone with them. Then, from the other side of the roof, Warrior heard the screams. He picked the boy up in his arms, lifting him high above the snowdrifts that reached past Warrior's waist and above the boy's head, and ran through the snow in the direction of the screams.

The woman was bloodied and bruised, but the hardness in her eyes told a tale that her body did not. She had struggled and though the men had just overcome her, they knew they had been in a battle; that they had warred. They had her body bent over one of the exhaust pipes of the incinerator, her jacket, violently ripped from her, lay discarded in the snow, and her dress was shredded. One man held her down, and the other stood behind her, his hands reaching up under her dress. Warrior took the boy from his arms and placed him down in the snow. His jaw tightened and his eyes closed to near slits as he looked at the woman's face. The man whose hands held her down was pushing the side of her head into the metal pipe. Her face was turned toward Warrior, and her eyes watched him, silently. Warrior gritted his teeth and breathed in deeply, one word flooding his mind:

*No . . .*

Warrior was on top of the men before they even saw him. He threw the one who was holding the woman off her with such force that as he stumbled to regain his footing, his head smashed into the brick wall and he fell down, unconscious. Warrior grabbed the other man whose hand had been under the woman's dress, gripped him by his coat, lifted him in the air, and slammed his head down onto the metal pipe. Warrior was so close to the man that he could smell the sweat frozen on the man's skin, and could see in his cold eyes that had so recently been filled with power but now were glazed, full of fear. He lifted him up and carried him toward the roof's edge. The man feebly attempted to fight Warrior's grip, but it was fastened with iron, and there was no freedom to be found from these chains. As Warrior held the man high in the air, he heard the woman's voice from behind him.

"No. He's mine." Her words were spoken slowly, making them that much more dangerous. Warrior turned around, still holding the man's body, and looked at the woman.

The brown skin of her face was bloodied, and one eye was badly swollen, but her long and powerful body moved with strength and purpose. She came over toward Warrior, and without even looking in his direction she took the man from his arms. Her face was set in a stiff mask as blood slowly dripped down one of her high, chiseled cheekbones. The only thing that the mask could not cover was the fierce line of her tightened lips. The man she held had ceased to struggle as soon as she had gripped him, knowing that now his fate was sealed. As she looked the man in his face one last time, Warrior swore that he saw her lips turn ever so slightly into a smile. The woman thrust the man out over the roof, his feet hanging in the cold air, and then she released him. The man fell down toward the dark alley below, his brief cries ending suddenly.

The woman stood at the roof's edge for a long time, doing nothing but looking down. Her body was completely still, her head bowed, as she looked into the darkness of the alley. Finally, her searching done, the woman brought her head up, turned around, and looked at Warrior. She made no sound, but she was crying, the tears running down her blood-streaked face. She walked slowly over to Warrior and took his hand. She looked into his eyes and said, through a taut jaw, "Yes."

She walked away, stopping only to pick up her torn jacket. As she moved toward the staircase that led from the roof, she walked through Warrior's footprints in the snow. She passed by the boy who was still standing in the spot where Warrior had placed him, and though she was close enough to reach out and touch him, she walked right by as if she could not see him. After the woman disappeared from Warrior's sight, the boy walked slowly toward Warrior and took hold of his hand, wrapping his own hand around his fingertips. Solemnly, he led Warrior to the edge of the roof and then stopped, releasing Warrior's hand.

When Warrior reached the edge, he saw that the man who had been thrown by the woman was hanging on, nearly twenty feet down, grasping a piece of metal that jutted out from the building, slowly slipping on its icy surface. The man looked up at Warrior.

"Please . . . please?" the man pleaded as he slipped further.

The boy reached up as the man spoke and took hold of Warrior's hand. Suddenly, Warrior's mind was filled with visions. He saw brotherman lying in a pool of blood on the street. He heard the sounds of brotherman's skull breaking and his teeth being shattered by the barrel of a gun. He was a man. Warrior saw a boy filled with the wonder of new sights and visions, a boy who looked out at the world with innocence. Then Warrior saw darkness. He saw a boy with beautiful brown eyes that served as guides to undiscovered dreams. Then Warrior saw nothing. Warrior saw the back of a blue soldier's car, and feet pounding away at a child's face. He saw blood everywhere. He was a boy. Warrior saw a shadow taking the hand of a lost girl, leading her into a darkened alley. She would be his meal. He heard her moans, desperate sounds of pain and confusion. He felt her fear and she wondered where her mother was. She was a girl. Warrior saw a woman's brown skin against the snow. She was bent over a pipe, her body exhausted from the struggle. The violation so extreme he felt as the madness descended on her. She was a woman.

As the visions left Warrior, he looked down at the boy. The boy tilted his head back and turned his face toward Warrior. Then, the boy slowly opened his shut eyelids and showed Warrior where his eyes had once been. Warrior looked into the raw, empty holes, and the rage flowed. He could only hear beating drums. How can someone do this to another human body? Warrior stood there, watching, as the man slowly lost his grip on the icy metal.

"Please. You have to help me," again he pleaded, his hands almost at the end of the broken pipe.

Warrior gently placed his hand on the head of the boy who now stood in front of him, leaning against Warrior's legs. And they watched.

The man fell into the darkness below. They sat together in the snow, until the last remnants of the sun's light had faded away, until the moon shone brightly in the night's sky. In silence, they looked down at the chaos that still filled the streets, and at the occasional calm that descended, its stillness filled only with darting shadows. They heard the screams, the crackling radios of blue soldiers, and the sirens. They heard the voices calling out, and they heard the wailing of the wolves. Warrior and the boy watched and listened.

◙ ◙ ◙

Once again Warrior stood on the steps of the stoop and blood ran through the street, like a river. He stood alone, the boy having disappeared as they walked down the stairs from the rooftop. They had walked through the darkness, the boy once again leading the way, clenching Warrior's hand, guiding him. As they reached the foot of the stairs, the boy released Warrior's hand. Warrior called out to the boy, blindly stumbling through the rubble-filled rooms, but there was no use. The boy was gone. Now, Warrior stood alone on the stoop as the river of blood flowed past him.

The wolves were all around him, lining the bank of the river. Warrior thought for a moment they had come to feed, to drink from its depths until he heard one sustained howl, one wolf crying out desperately, and for the first time, Warrior truly heard the call. The wolf was not crying out for food, he was being held captive, and seeing the river's powerful current, he was deciding whether he would be carried away to his long-desired freedom. The wolves had never been searching for food, they had never been following Warrior out of hunger, they were being driven by the demons, the same ones who endlessly tracked Warrior The wolves were crying out for their release.

Warrior heard the bottomless laugh of the claw, and as he listened to the laugh, he heard the whip of the claw's demon kin descend, driving the wolves from the river's edge. They had come to witness the chaos that was their creation. As his pack fled at the cracking of the whip, the lone, howling wolf pointed his nose toward the sky and let out one last haunted cry—then leapt into the bloody river. As Warrior watched the river's current carry the wolf away, he was overcome by the sound of drums that beat violently, almost too fast, and as the speaker's hands struck them, they screamed.

Warrior ran. He ran from the sight of the river and from the sound of the wolves who once again were locked in their cage. He ran from the demons who called after him with whispers, laughing, mocking,

*Run, Warrior, run . . . run . . . run . . .*

He ran past the blue soldiers and their red and blue swirling lights, paying no mind to their calls to stop, his powerful legs carrying him quickly out of their reach. He ran through snow-banks, over shattered glass, and past burning buildings. He ran through dark blocks, turning corners blindly, staying close to the buildings, away from the streetlights, in the shadows. As he ran, he pulled up his black hood over his already covered head, and melted into the darkness. He ran past alleys, and past buildings out of which poured music. Past night walkers, past still open corner stores, past children playing in the snow, and the elders who watched them from windows, Warrior ran. He ran, and ran, and ran.

He reached a subway station, grabbed hold of the railing, and fled down the stairs. His chest heaving, the sweat feeling good on his chilled skin, Warrior looked down the tracks, and seeing the two bright white lights winding through the darkened tunnel, he breathed deeply, relieved that the train was coming. When it came to a stop in front of him, the doors opened, and he walked into the empty train and sat down. He pulled his hood on tighter, the sides serving as blinders, hiding his face from other eyes. He tried to quiet the pounding in his head and his heavy breathing, but it was no use. The train snaked out of the station and sped toward Brooklyn.

◙ ◙ ◙

Warrior stepped inside the brownstone, then turned to shut the mighty oakwood door behind him. It was warm inside, and Warrior could hear all of the familiar sounds that filled the house. He could hear his father moving around, upstairs, most likely searching through the unending piles of books, records, and song sheets that littered the floor or, filing through the two massive steel file cabinets whose towering presence rose up from the floor to the ceiling. Within its deep drawers were old family photographs, childhood drawings, school report cards, long ago sent letters, deeds to Southern lands, and freedom papers—all the carefully kept history of a family. Warrior heard his father moving around and imagined him sitting at the foot of one of the files, surrounded by yellowed papers, remembering.

The sound that was heard above all others, the one that claimed the air, was, as usual, music, or as his father always said, "voice." This night, the word was being passed by Coltrane. His horn told tales of worlds only he had seen, worlds others doubted even existed, but Trane knew. Warrior walked up the stairs to the second floor, leaning heavily on the banister. As he moved, he heard Trane, and the drums that filled his own ears joined the cry of the horn in kinship, sharing a conversation that some had named, a name Warrior had no need for, having long ago decided just to listen. His father was playing his favorite piece of music, one that merged love and the sanctified, two songs that merged into one, "Pursuance" and "Psalm," from the spiritual journey called *A Love Supreme.* Warrior knew it well.

He walked into what had once been his room, and felt peaceful—though the walls were bare, all of his possessions having been moved to Harlem. For him, this room was still the deepest part of home. Even in its starkness, it held many memories, it felt safe and familiar. The dark-stained furniture was the same, the walls were still winter green, the old, thick brown drapes hung low, sealing off all light from outside, and the bedspread made of the same material, but a more earthy shade of dusty red brown, still covered the small, sunken bed. At the head of the bed, on the night table, was the one picture that remained. It had been taken the day Warrior's mother had come home with his sister from the hospital. His mother was in her bed, dressed in a white nightgown, tired but glowing,

holding her daughter against her breast with one arm, as Warrior's father, smiling from ear to ear, lay on the bed with her,
one hand resting gently on his daughter's head, one wrapped
around his wife. Warrior was not looking at the camera, stared
wide-eyed at his sister, leaning on the end of the bed, his mother's hand in his.

Warrior took off his jeans and his sweatshirt, keeping his
undershirt on. Earlier in the day, the cold had given him a deep
chill and he still hadn't recovered; in fact, it had gotten worse,
now he was shivering. The room was warm, since his father
always kept the heat on high, so warm that it felt almost damp
as the heat fought the cold that raged just outside the windows.
He closed the door, needing silence. He pulled back the cover
and climbed into bed. As he lay in the dark room, his lungs
heaved, desperately seeking air. In the silence, he heard only
the sounds of the beating of the drums. The speaker's hands
had lost control, and the drums pulsed wildly. There was no
rhythm. No order. No time.

# CHAPTER 7

W arrior's father, surrounded by his papers, had fallen asleep on the couch. He had spent hours reconstructing the family tree, the passing years having stolen some of the names and stories from his memory. He needed the memories of family elders in order to extend back to the years before Emancipation, but even they hadn't known all of the history of past generations, slavery having erased  dates and names. Through the night, he struggled to reclaim those lost in name, and to restore the ties of blood that had been dissolved by time. When his eyes had grown weary, Warrior's father had simply closed them and slowly faded into a deep sleep, his prone body covered by papers, his mind having gone somewhere else, captivated by the world of Trane that floated through the speakers on the second floor.

It was not until morning came that he knew that his son was in the house.

He woke, sat up from the couch, and with a sigh, placed the materials that had served him in his struggle the night before back in their resting place, to be kept safe until another time. Inside the drawers of the metal files he placed the family diaries with their dates of birth, marriages, and deaths, scribbled carefully in the margins. Inside the drawers he placed the registration papers that had been pulled from the records of the Freedmen's Bureau decades ago. There too were the old deeds to lands that since their issue had passed through many hands, and by many means; in deals brought about by grand dreams of a better life, in bets lost in late night card games played by the light of kerosene lamps, at tables filled with too much moonshine and too little sense, and in agreements signed by the force of burning crosses and creaking ropes. Into these metal drawers, along with these documents, was the town census dated from just before the beginning of the war, and the manumission papers from the days when blood was owned. He returned these things to their place, a few more names added to the legacy, having been rediscovered from their dry pages of faded ink.

It was when Warrior's father walked downstairs to make breakfast that he saw, past his own room, that Warrior's childhood bedroom door was closed. He walked down the long hallway and pushed opened the door. During the coldest months of winter, the heat of the house expanded the wood and the swelling caused the door to stick. As he pushed the door open he felt the hot air on his face. The room was dark, and the air was damp with sweat. Warrior was in his bed, under the covers, curled up, as if he had not yet come into this world.

He didn't think it was strange that his son was there. Warrior often dropped by without notice. In fact, that was the way he had raised him. Family doesn't need to call, they just come by and make themselves at home. What bothered him was that Warrior hadn't woken him when he had come in, hadn't even let him know that he was in the house. He walked over to the bed to wake Warrior in order to ask if he wanted breakfast. School had once again been canceled, the snow having been too much to clear in a day. When he placed his hand on Warrior's arm he felt the heat of his son's blood. Having raised two children, Warrior's father knew a fever when he felt one. He shook Warrior, his concern showing in the force he used, and when Warrior only responded with incoherent moans, his father became more concerned.

Warrior was sick, and if he had come to Brooklyn without telling his mother and then slept through the night, she would be frantic. Warrior's father recalled what he had been doing throughout the day and into the evening, during the hours before he had become involved with piecing together the family history. He had been playing his bass and composing new pieces on the piano and had been in that creative space that artists can sometimes enter, and not wanting to be disturbed, he had unplugged the phone. He tried to wake Warrior again, and getting no response, he went into the living room to search for the phone. He pulled it from underneath one of the piles of books that were stacked near the piano, plugged in the cord and called Warrior's mother.

She had been awake all night. She had called hospitals and the blue soldiers' headquarters, but after a long and painful debate with herself she had refrained from calling the morgue.

Earlier she had spent most of the day in the park with her daughter, laughing, and even crying once or twice, having to reassure her worried child that the tears were due to the cold, knowing in truth, that they were from the joy of watching her child's spirit at play. They had ice skated and when they had gotten cold, had gone for a warm lunch. After eating they had walked through the park to the museum just outside of the park's walls. They had spent hours walking the halls, viewing the exhibits, her daughter full of questions, she full of answers that she enjoyed sharing. After her daughter had become tired, they took the train back Uptown.

It was when they had walked up from the station and come out into the cold streets, that she had felt the tension in the air. Moving through the neighborhood, she observed that the streets were too quiet, too empty, and realized that there had been trouble. She gripped her daughter's hand tightly and pulled her along as they quickly walked home. When they neared their building, she had seen that blue soldiers were roaming, buildings were burning, and broken glass was everywhere. While they were gone, the neighborhood had exploded. Someone, somewhere, had been pushed too far, and now people were pushing back. As she walked down her street, the voice in her mind told her that Warrior had been involved in the explosion, and feeling dread all around her, she had rushed through the front door and up the stairs to her apartment. When she opened the door, she had immediately called out Warrior's name. Only to be met by silence.

After a few hours of concealing her worry from her daughter and telling herself that Warrior would be back soon, she had put her daughter to bed, closed the door tightly, and walked into the kitchen. She filled the teakettle with water and waited for it to boil. After putting a filter in the coffeepot and carefully measuring the scoops of ground coffee beans, adding one more than usual, she sat down. As she sat at the kitchen table, staring through the living room and to the window, she had placed her hands together and tried to massage away the ache in her palms. After a few minutes that brought no relief, she stopped and began to gently stroke her fingers, while continuing to stare into the darkness.

The whistle of the teakettle interrupted her thoughts and she walked to the stove, to brew the coffee. While lost in her thoughts, she slowly removed the morning newspaper from the table, stacked the mail, neatly, on the counter, and wiped down the wood of the table with a damp sponge, restoring its perfectly kept finish. She poured a cup of the steaming coffee and sat back down. As she carefully wiped a spot on the table with her finger, a spot the sponge had missed, the phone had rung, and she had answered it on the first ring. It wasn't Warrior.

It was some hours later, after calling the house in Brooklyn yet again and still getting no answer, that she called the local headquarters of the blue soldiers. After countless rings, a man had answered the phone who spoke in rushed words and shortened sentences. He had told her that Warrior was not there, but after a day like today, there was no telling where her son might be. Then he had added quickly that she might want to try the hospital, or the morgue. Before she had time to release her rage, he had knowingly hung up the phone, and she was left to scream at a dial tone.

Then she had begun to call the hospitals. After hours of being put on hold or being transferred, she was repeatedly told by each hospital that Warrior was not there. Finally she had heard a voice which sounded like it wanted to help, a voice that though it had no answers wished that it did. The nurse sounded like she was in her fifties, and the rhythm of her speech told of a Caribbean birth, her tone revealed the shared experiences of motherhood. She told Warrior's mother that it was a horrible night, that most of those who had been hurt had come to her hospital, and that none were Warrior. She said that many of those who had been admitted were just young boys who arrived with bruised bodies and beaten faces and still others, even worse, riddled with bullets. It was still early, she said, and already it had been one of the worst nights in her twenty-nine years as a nurse. She repeated the word, *cha-os*, telling Warrior's mother once again that most of the injured and the dead had already been brought in, and that Warrior was not among them, she swore that she would call, immediately, if anyone fitting Warrior's description arrived. Warrior's mother sat by the phone until dawn.

When the phone finally rang, it rang once. Then twice. Then three times. She slowly picked up the receiver and brought it to her ear, closed her eyes, and bit her lower lip until it bled. The voice on the other end of the line was Warrior's father, who said that Warrior was with him in Brooklyn and was very sick. She hung up, rushed into her daughter's room, wrapped her sleeping child in her blankets and carried her out the door. She walked outside and hailed a livery cab whose company sticker bore the name *Malcolm*, and told the driver to drive to Brooklyn, quick.

The driver was about to object to the trip from a neighborhood so many outsiders feared to yet another, but when he looked in his rearview mirror and saw how rigid her face was set as she anticipated his words, he decided to drive on.

When Warrior's father opened the heavy, oak wood door, she searched his eyes and saw the worry and the pain that he tried to hide. They embraced, their daughter's sleeping body pressed between them, as they both leaned on each other, trying to absorb some of the other's strength. After removing her coat and shoes, they walked up the stairs together and down the hallway to the room that had once been theirs. She placed their daughter on the bed and then he pulled the covers up around her small shoulders, molding the quilt to their daughter's body so that she would be warm. They walked down the hallway, and when they reached the door to Warrior's room, he rested his hand on her shoulder and pushed the door open for her.

Warrior was dripping with sweat now, lying on his stomach, absolutely still. His mother walked over to him, reached down and placed her hand on the back of his neck. His skin felt like it was on fire. She pulled the covers back and felt his undershirt. It was soaked. Warrior's father held up his son's body as she removed Warrior's underclothes, leaving him naked. Then she stripped the bed of its sheets, pillowcases, and blanket, bundled them up and placed them on the floor. She walked over to the closet in the room, and from its shelves took down some clean bedding. She made the bed with soft, tight-fitting sheets, and thin cotton pillowcases that smelled of lemon. Warrior's father placed his son on the bed, gently placing his head on the pillows. Warrior didn't make a sound as he was moved, but once he was back on the bed, his body curled up again, as if it was the only position that brought him any comfort.

Warrior's mother went to the bathroom and returned with a bottle of rubbing alcohol. She rolled up her sleeves, cupped one hand, and filling it with alcohol, she began to rub Warrior's body, trying to get her fingers under his burning skin. Warrior's father leaned in the doorway, watching. He remembered that she had always massaged Warrior like this when he was young, when he had fevers or childhood pains. She would spend hours leaning over his body, armed only with alcohol and her hands. She would rub his legs, his shoulders, his neck, his arms, never stopping until she was convinced that she had rubbed away all the pain. Warrior always fell asleep as she performed her task, and when he woke, whether he had a fever or just been sore, he would always smile and say, "All better, Mommy." As she repeated this familiar healing ritual, Warrior's father watched, knowing that as always, she would not rest until her son's pain was gone.

He walked to the closet, took down a thick flannel cover from the top shelf and placed it at the foot of the bed. He knew that when she was done, she would want to cover Warrior with something to sweat out the fever. He looked at his son once more, and as he turned to leave the room he smiled through his pain, knowing that the fever would no longer be allowed to run its course unchallenged. The alcohol was fighting the sweat that poured from Warrior's body, and his mother's hands were battling whatever it was that raged inside of him.

He walked into the living room, and not knowing what else

to do, he picked up his bass that leaned against the bookshelf, sat down on his favorite stool, brought his hands up to the strings, and freed the voices.

The bass moaned. At first it was slow and sorrowful, the kind of deep moan heard at Southern funerals, cried out by grieving mothers dressed in black, the moan of women who have seen their children buried times before, placed in the ground and covered with soil. Women who know this ritual like they know their name, women to whom black dresses are a second skin. Women who cry out in an endless wail, a sound heard long after their mouths have closed. A sound that has no beginning, and no end.

But then the moan picked up speed. Warrior's father's hands made the bass scream, and scream. It became a wail of one who had lost his mind. It became a wail voiced in a language of another kind. Like a Jazz scatter gone mad. The words made no sense when they stood alone. They flowed together, one on top of the next, the speaker never pausing, not even breaking to take a breath, but then, when his words finally ended, when the last note was said, the speaker exhaled deeply and laughed, for as he had uttered his last word, it had been like the completion of a circle, and it had all made sense, and the listener had smiled, nodding, finally understanding his word.

Warrior's father found comfort in this world. He held conversations with the voices, speaking with his bass, calling out to them for answers. He played furiously, sliding his hands up and down the wood of the bass, slapping it with force like a drum when he felt the need, making the metal strings screech with each riff, playing until his fingers bled. The blood feeling good, and hearing the echo of the notes he had driven from the bass calling out that he had played the way it was meant to be played, he had placed his fingers back on the strings and continued the conversation.

Warrior's mother sat looking down at her son, gently stroking his face with the back of her hand. The sounds of the bass had poured into the room for hours, and as she had listened she had continued to drive the fever from her son's body. When his skin began to feel cooler after her hands had grown too tired to continue, she stood up from the bed and spread the flannel cover over his still sweating body. After tucking the blanket under him to seal in the heat, she sat back down on the bed to watch over her son. As she looked down at his sleeping face, she noticed that his eyes were completely closed. She would watch him for two days.

▣ ▣ ▣

*I stand in a graveyard, thinking of the thousands of Black children who have died in the war of my generation. I think of those who have passed away too young. I stand in their new home.*

*It is an old country cemetery that extends out from an overgrown forest, about a quarter of a mile back from the meeting of two dusty dirt roads. Where the roads lead to, I don't know, I can't see that from where I stand. All I know is that they cross, and then continue, for as far as my eyes can see. I face the forest, at the edge of the graveyard. In each of the other directions there is nothing but barren land and the endless roads.*

*The cemetery is overrun by flowers, and by life. Gnarled trees* rise from the earth, their dense branches casting great shadows. It is the only graveyard I have ever been in where I feel the presence of light, of warmth. It is not cold and gray. It does not serve as the keeper of the distant dead. It is the resting place of worn bodies, and the playground of souls. I can feel a pulsating spirit of life. The ground is alive, and the children are singing.

The gravestones though, reveal otherwise. Out of the forest they appear like a wave; from how deep within I don't know. The forest cannot hold them. They have broken through the trees and extend to the road. They stand in perfect rows, stiff, like proud soldiers. The first lines have just been planted, and are marked by names and dates, recently carved into stone. As I walk along the path from the road to the forest, passing each row I feel the eyes of those named watching me, wondering why I walk among them. As they watch, the drums keep time, counting the souls as they arrive. From the forest's depths, emerging from the shadows three figures appear. A man. A woman. A boy.

The man is tall, slightly taller than I am, and thin as sugar-cane. His skin is blue-black, and the way it tightly covers his long muscles makes his stark white beard and matted gray hair seem out of place. He moves like a wolf, as if he can pounce at will. The red and black tattoo on his neck announces such a deadly man. As he sits down among the graves, I see the scars that reach up from his back, clawing at his bare shoulders. Dead skin that tells the tale of another time. He watches me as I walk toward him, searching, judging. His eyes are the color of ebony, and filled with the pain of a man who has seen, and now passes the word. I remember eyes that brought a midnight so dark that they erased a man's mind. Eyes that looked into souls. Eyes that screamed *of pain and warned of retribution. I can feel them inside me, drawing me near.*

*The boy runs up to me, his face covered in a smile. I know the smile . . . but not the boy. He has a big, bullet-shaped head that seems too large for his neck, like it belongs to a boy twice his age. As he grabs my hand, he laughs as only children laugh, filled with absolute joy. He pulls me toward the man, insistently; as if it is a game I must play. As he runs in front of me, tugging on my arm, he looks back and smiles even more, seeing that now I am smiling too. I look into his huge, brown, deeply set eyes and realize why he is so familiar, and why I could not recognize him. I had forgotten what he looked like with eyes.*

*The woman walks slowly from the forest and sits on a tree stump that rises up from the ground, among the graves. She walks with a strong and powerful stride. As she sits down, she unwinds the long white cloth that is wrapped around her body, releasing her sleeping child from her back. As she moves the infant boy from his resting place, the baby opens his eyes and looks at his mother. She holds the child against her breast, and he quickly falls back asleep, and the sound of his breathing fills the air of the cemetery. As she looks up from her sleeping son and into my face, there is something that is said in the way she lifts her chin. My ears fill with Kila's song.*

*Now other voices come. The demons?*

*"No. There are no demons here. They do not have the power to show their face in this place. They took us in life Warrior, not here. We can't fight them in your world, but we can serve as the blood of your testimony. You are the witness, Warrior, pass the word. If for*

*no other reason than for us . . . Memory is somethin' powerful, it has served us before, it'll serve us again. Listen now, hear, he speaks of the power of remembering . . ."*

*It was the rumbling of countless voices.*

*Now the man is in my head. "We came here in chains. We came here as slaves, owned by another's hand. We came here naked, with nothing but our blood and our minds. We created a people on memory. You hear? Memory. So what do you know, Warrior? What are your memories?"*

*I allow my mind to wander, to fly back to childhood, to try to remember what has been stolen. It has been so long since I have dreamed, I have lost so many of my memories. The demons have filled my mind, and often I have thought of nothing else. The demons have made sure that I did not dream. Yeah, Daddy, a bitter pill to swallow.*

*I hear a voice in my head responding to the man's question, but it is not mine. The boy speaks, but it is my memories he speaks of. Mine. Now the voice is familiar. The boy speaks in my voice from long ago. It is the voice of "Little Warrior." It is my voice, and it is his. Here, he is who I was. In life he is a lesson: This is what they do to witnesses who use their eyes. He remembers what has been lost to me.*

*"My daddy tol' me that when we was taken over from Africa ta here, that some a us jumped off the ship so we wouldn't have ta be slaves. He say there's thousands a bones on the bottom a the ocean floor. He say the people who left them bones was the real warriors.*

*That what he say. You think they passed on to be with they Gods? Or you think they souls are with those bones? And what about us? You think they forgave us? For forgettin' 'em and all? You think they still claim us? You think when we pass on, they'll be there… waitin'? I hope so . . . I really do. But when I ask my mommy and daddy, they say they don't know. And when I ask the voices, they don't never answer."*

*The man returned to my mind. "And what about now, Warrior, what answers to your questions have you found?"*

*It is my voice that speaks now. "In this life that we live, those who survive and those named in stone, there are more questions than answers. We have seen so much pain, but then they tell us that we are the ones who are supposed to be free. You survived the Passage, lived through slavery times, and brought Jim Crow to his knees, but it's my generation that's dying. And when we bury each other, when the blood runs in the streets around us, when we struggle every day of our lives with the demons, and when we feel lost in the pain, it's then that I still wonder, what ever happened to my Gods in Africa."*

*The man's voice responds. "And so some a you discard your skin, thinkin' that'll bring answers."*

*And I say, "You know better than us its force, what it can drive us to do. It's a sickness, a plague that taints our blood, causing us to forget as the rage drives us blind. We forget where we've come from, we forget our kin. We forget how many have struggled, and how much blood has been lost. For four hundred years we have been taught that our lives are not worth living, and many of us have learned well. Our people have all faced demons since we came here, but this has been the one that has always been there, the one all generations have had to battle. Because of the color of our skin, we are who we are. It's why it's so."*

*Now the woman's voice enters my mind. "It opens your eyes to the truth. And once they are opened, the seer either goes crazy, a mind lost in the face of such terror, or becomes a warrior and learns the lesson of the slaves: To find the island of your mind, a place their hatred can't never reach. The hatred of our skin is strong, can make us hate ourselves, but once we come to know the strength of our blood, once we look this hatred in the eye and let it be known that we will not be its creation, that it will not steal our minds, then there is nothin' that we can't survive. The hatred of our skin has a mighty power. It takes us into the world of rage and of pain that it has created, and we are forced to seek to survive. It brings you into this world, but it also is the only thing that can bring you out. It opens your eyes. What you do with that vision is up to you."*

*And I speak to her. "And what about those who have lost their eyes? What about those who have had their minds stolen? Look around you, who do you think has sent all of these children here? Blindness is killing a generation. We kill each other, but all we have to do is look in the mirror to see that we are killing ourselves. I can't run from these killers of blood, I can't be afraid, 'cause they me. But I wonder, if they that lost, then, then they ain't blood no more. Right? And I can't carry my own steel to take their lives, 'cause then the chaos wins. And the pain of doing it, I think, the pain of killing blood, of letting the voices win, making me one of the wolves, would kill me.*

*And she says, "And so you are ready to spread the word? To speak for those who have been silenced?"*

*"Yes."*

*She looks down at her sleeping baby and then raises her eyes to meet mine. Her eyes are hard.*

*"You give your word, on the life of my child?"*

*"Yes."*

*The man's voice speaks of demons. "And when they come to make war with you? When they try to send you to the same fate as those of your generation who have departed, when they try to silence the witness, what then? They strong boy, they like wild dogs that never rest. They even almost made you try to fly. What happens when their voices come a callin', and they seek to drive you from the path?"*

*And I say, "They've called and I've declared war, they know where I stand. At one time I was sure that I wouldn't survive. Now I know that I must. It is a hard path to walk, but it's my only choice. It's the path of survival. When the rage comes, the path serves as my answer. The path is what has the power to bring me out, to show me the way. Without it, the madness comes, and the line between those who are strong and those who lose their minds is thin. I know, I've been there. As for those who do cross the line, maybe they've just seen too much, and decided to fly away. But there's no way that I can ever lose my way. Too many voices serve as my guides. Too much blood is with me. I am not a man. I am history, walking."*

*He nods. She smiles as she rocks her child in her arms. The boy looks at me, and I see myself. Then she speaks. "Go now, your blood is waiting . . ."*

*As I walk from the edge of the trees toward the crossing of the roads, I weave through the path of gravestones. As I walk among them, I hear their voices rumbling. It is a scream. It is a cry. It is a demand. Those named in stone call out aching to be heard.*

*At the meeting of the dusty roads at the edge of the graveyard, I can still hear the chorus of voices calling out. I still hear the children singing, and the visions of the man, the woman, and the boy run through my mind, echoing in my memory. But as I near the Crossroads, the voices fall silent and the singing fades, and then there is only one sound that I hear. It is the beating of the drum. Keeping time. Counting off the souls as they continue to arrive.*

Warrior opened his eyes, saw the Gods around him, and remembered all of his dreams.

## ACKNOWLEDGMENTS

There were two women who fell in love with *Passage* and ushered it through the process—Susan L. Taylor and Marie Brown. Thank you, Susan, for all of your support and faith in this work and for connecting me to Marie. Marie, my agent and editor, I appreciate all of your careful attention to *Passage* and your commitment to the vision. You both always understood the story.

I would like to thank Dan Simon, the founder and publisher of Seven Stories Press. I will always be thankful to Dan for wanting *Passage* to be a member of the Seven Stories family of books—and for his deep belief in this novel. Thank you as well to Ruth Weiner, Lauren Hooker, Sanina Clark, and all the dedicated staff at Seven Stories Press for their passionate support of *Passage*. I would also like to acknowledge Rodrigo Corral for the striking and evocative cover design he created.

As always, thank you to my brother, Adam Lazarre-White, the fiercely talented artist; to my grandmother Lois Meadows White and in loving memory of my great-uncle Alphonso Meadows Sr., the tellers of the family stories and legacy that inspired much of this work; to my father, Douglas Hughes White, the historian who instilled in me his passion for seeking answers and struggling with what one finds; and to my mother, Jane Lazarre, my first and always best writing teacher, the one who taught me to love the word.

*Khary Lazarre-White*

# ABOUT THE AUTHOR

Khary Lazarre-White is a writer, social justice advocate, attorney, and activist who has dedicated his life to the educational outcome and opportunities for young people of color at key life stages. His support base is far-reaching and diverse, built over the past twenty-two years as co-founder and executive director of The Brotherhood/Sister Sol. He has received awards for his work, including the Oprah Winfrey Angel Network Use Your Life Award, the Ford Foundation Leadership for a Changing World Award, awards from Black Girls Rock! and the Andrew Goodman Foundation, and a Resident Fellowship Award to the Rockefeller Foundation's Bellagio Center. Khary Lazarre-White is a highly influential presence among national policymakers and broadcast, print, and social media outlets. He has written for the *Huffington Post*, NYU Press, Nation Books, and MSNBC.com, and has edited three books, *The Brotherhood Speaks*, *Voices of the Brotherhood/Sister Sol*, and *Off the Subject*. He lives in Harlem. *Passage* is his first novel.

# ABOUT SEVEN STORIES PRESS

Seven Stories Press is an independent book publisher based in New York City. We publish works of the imagination by such writers as Nelson Algren, Russell Banks, Octavia E. Butler, Ani DiFranco, Assia Djebar, Ariel Dorfman, Coco Fusco, Barry Gifford, Martha Long, Luis Negrón, Hwang Sok-yong, Lee Stringer, and Kurt Vonnegut, to name a few, together with political titles by voices of conscience, including Subhankar Banerjee, the Boston Women's Health Collective, Noam Chomsky, Angela Y. Davis, Human Rights Watch, Derrick Jensen, Ralph Nader, Loretta Napoleoni, Gary Null, Greg Palast, Project Censored, Barbara Seaman, Alice Walker, Gary Webb, and Howard Zinn, among many others. Seven Stories Press believes publishers have a special responsibility to defend free speech and human rights, and to celebrate the gifts of the human imagination, wherever we can. In 2012 we launched Triangle Square books for young readers with strong social justice and narrative components, telling personal stories of courage and commitment. For additional information, visit www.sevenstories.com